DRAGON'S LOVE

RED PLANET DRAGONS OF TAJSS BOOK THREE

MIRANDA MARTIN

CONTENTS

ABOUT THIS BOOK

I guess I'm one of the last survivors of the human race and I'm stranded on this hell of a desert alien planet. Sucks to be me.

Our ship crashed months ago and those of us left are struggling to survive the boiling heat in barbaric living conditions. The only reason we're not all dead is one of my friends got knocked up by a native alien and he lets us live in his ruined city. We should be grateful but a lot of the humans hate the dragons and the girls who mate with them. Fools.

The natives are huge, seven foot tall dragon-men with wings and tails and scales. Surly and overly protective, who needs that? Not me. Alien baby fever is the new in thing, but I'm not falling for the hype. I've always survived being alone and I don't need anyone to change that. Try telling that to Shidan, the most annoyingly persistent alien male around.

Thanks to the primitive nature of the destroyed planet we have no idea what's happening when things go wrong with my friend's pregnancy. I'm sure I can salvage something from our crashed ship that will help, but to get there I'll have to leave the city's protection and go out in the sweltering heat where everything wants to kill me. The only way I'll survive is if Shidan comes too and he's made it clear he wants only one thing. Love.

AMARA

Stubborn, stubborn machine! I can't get this motor to run. The wrench slips and my knuckles scrape against metal.

"Damn it!" I yell, dropping the wrench and grabbing my injured hand with the other.

Pain throbs in time with the beating of my heart. I hate this, hate this place, hate my new job, I hate every damn thing about all of it. Seven months ago my friends and I crashed on this barren wasteland of a planet. It's totally hell even if we like to joke about it and argue if it's more like Star Wars or Star Trek. This place sucks. It's hot and sand gets in places I didn't even know I had.

We live in what was once a great city but now is little more than a ruin. The building we're in was, maybe, once the city's power source but now it's a decaying jumble of machines and metal. It's big and smells old, like rust and mold. There's barely enough light to work by streaming in from rotted gaps in the high ceiling. Dancing from foot to foot I wait for the pain to subside.

"Are you okay?" Inga asks, over my shoulder.

"Do I look like I'm okay?" I snap.

"I'm sorry, I…" she trails off.

Great, I'm being a total bitch to my friends, again. Sometimes I can't seem to stop myself. "Hey," I say to Inga's retreating form. "I'm sorry. I'm a bitch. It's just hot and damn it this hurt, bad." I hold my hand up between us, the scraped knuckles still red.

"It's cool," she says. "Scotty used to yell at the rest of the engineers too."

She grins with the reference but all I can muster is a wan smile. I'm not an engineer, I'm a pilot. What good is that though? We need pilots like I need a hole in my head. There's nothing to fly so a pilot does nothing to increase our odds of survival. On the ship that was our home, I hung out enough on the flight deck to pick up a few things from the real engineers, but none of them survived so I'm the best we've got. Hence, I'm pressed into service as an engineer. Which I'm not but I'm doing my best.

"What is wrong my lyutik?" Shidan asks, coming around the corner.

Shidan is a Zmaj, a native inhabitant of this desert hell. He showed up two months ago and has been following me around ever since.

I don't know how long ago, but there was a war the Zmaj call the Devastation. Before that this place was an advanced technological society. Something happened in the war that wiped out all but a handful of male Zmaj. It triggered some primal instinct that drove them apart, they can't be near each other without trying to establish dominance so now they live like barbarians.

They're dragon-men, literal seven-foot tall, enormous dragon-men. Shidan is covered head to toe in rusty-brown scales edged with red-blue. They're thicker along his backside and a lot lighter on the front. He even has wings and a tail. Like all the Zmaj, he runs around shirtless, exposing his over defined abs and chest muscles that are enough to turn any girl's head. His face isn't really reptilian, it's much more human, but sharp and sculpted. I can't deny it's an attractive face with a strong jaw but he's always staring at me with clear, amber eyes. His hotness doesn't mean I like him stalking me.

"It's nothing," I reply in Zmaj, bending down to pick up the wrench I dropped.

There are a few hundred human survivors from our crashed generation ship living in the city and they're all counting on me to fix these damn motors. If I can figure it out, then we'll have electricity. Maybe. I think that's what these things do. Or they could turn on and fry us all. Summon a horde of zombies. Who knows?

"Ladon wants to know how it's going?" Shidan asks.

Ladon, this city belongs to him. How or why a single Zmaj can claim an entire city big enough to house hundreds of thousands if not millions seems to come back to the whole barbarian culture thing. Ladon is the first alien dragon-man we met. Through an act of fate, or luck, he fell in love with my friend Calista. If he hadn't, we'd probably be dead. This planet is the most inhospitable place I could imagine. Everything, and I mean everything, is trying to kill us. If the wildlife doesn't get you, the heat is unbearable and murders you slowly. Luckily, Calista got knocked up by her lover-boy-alien and so for her sake he deals with the rest of us survivors. Who knew our two species would be compatible? Not my area of expertise. Calista and Ladon struck a match, patient zero of an outbreak. A regular alien baby fever that's sweeping through the girls. Two other Zmaj showed up outside the city a while ago, one of them Shidan.

"Why is he always so stalkerish?" I ask Inga, speaking Common and glancing at Shidan.

3

Calista found a machine that taught humans how to speak and understand the Zmaj language but so far none of the Zmaj have learned Common.

"He's helping, remember?" she asks.

"I was being rhetorical."

"Oh, sorry," she gives me a sheepish smile to which I shake my head.

"I'm a pilot, not an engineer," I mutter in my best Scotty impression to make her happy, which sucks and I know it, but whatever.

"But you're great at it," Inga says.

I stare until I realize she's serious, then I feel awkward. "Thanks," I reply. She smiles and puts her attention back on the parts I have her cleaning.

Shidan stands close by, silently waiting for me to answer him. It's kind of creepy. He's always looking at me like that. If he was a guy, you know a normal human guy, I'd say he has puppy dog eyes. Like he's longing for me or something. Zmaj are weird that way. I've heard Ladon calling Calista his treasure. My other friend Jolie's Zmaj, Sverre, does the same thing. Hovering, being protective, looking out for her like she's too weak to do it on her own. I don't need or want anyone 'looking' out for me. I've spent my entire life proving myself. I'll stand on my own, I won't let anyone put themselves in harm's way because of me again.

"I'm glad he can't understand us. Why is he always looking at me like that?"

"He likes you," Inga insists, drying a piston with a towel.

"Well he can keep his like to himself," I mutter, putting the wrench back on the stubborn bolt that's refusing to let go.

Shidan comes closer and grabs for my hand. Instinctively I jerk away, my heart pounding so loud it's echoing in my ears, but I'm not fast enough. He catches my hand and pulls it up closer to his face. Carefully he inspects my scraped knuckles.

"You're injured," he observes.

"No shit, Sherlock," I say. "It's fine."

I try pulling my hand away again but I can't get out of his grip, it's too strong.

"Who is Sherlock? I am Shidan," he says, not letting my hand go.

He stares, looking down at me from his much greater height. His stunning eyes are a rich yellow that looks like a star burst. Shidan is smaller than the other Zmaj but he's still massive compared to me or pretty much any human. He's close, too close, a hint of an exotic scent fills my nose. The red-blue tinge of his scales seems to deepen. The wings on his back rustle and his tail switches side to side, his mouth tightening into a hard line. My mouth goes dry and I wonder what his lips taste like.

No! Push it aside. I will not kiss him. I'm not getting caught up in the alien baby fever Calista started. It's fine for them but I can make it on my own. I'm not letting anyone close ever again.

"I said it's fine," I reply, trying to tug my hand free.

"Let me cleanse it," he insists.

He pulls me along, gentle but insistent, until we're at the pail of water Inga's using as a cleaning tub. If I jerk my hand free, he'll let me go. I know because he's always doing things like this. Ever since he showed up outside the city's protective dome with that other Zmaj, Astarot, and fought tooth and nail over me. I think that's what pisses me off about them, they're possessive as hell. It's weird and while the other guy has moved on, Shidan makes sure he's always close. I can't turn around without bumping into him.

It's annoying, and cute, but more on the annoying side.

I'm not caught up in the fever. I'll tell myself that until it's true.

Shidan gently cleanses the scrape on my knuckles. He moves with deliberateness, pouring water over them then leaning in and inspecting. Apparently not satisfied he pours more water and inspects again before taking a clean towel and dabbing at the small wounds until they're dry. His warm breath passes over my skin and my core clenches with the first stirrings of desire. Now I jerk my hand free of his grip.

"I'm fine!" I yell in Common and he stares at me, confused. "I'm fine," I repeat myself in Zmaj so he'll understand.

"Good," he says.

"Do you think we'll be rescued?" Inga asks, giving me a welcome distraction.

"No."

"Oh," she says, her shoulders slumping.

"Look," I continue. "I know it's the popular thing to hope for, and there's the whole human first movement, or whatever stupid name they've come up with for their bigotry and xenophobia, but the fact is there's no one coming."

"How come?" she asks.

"Well look," I say. "We crashed almost eleven months ago. If a distress signal got out, which is doubtful, it has to reach Earth. Then Earth has to send a response team which will take more than our lifetime to arrive. We were the third generation on the ship that left Earth over one hundred years ago."

"Oh," she says, overwhelm heavy in her voice.

Way to go Amara. I hate feeling bad, especially when I'm telling the truth but what do I do now? I'm a pilot pretending to be an engineer. What do I know about comforting someone? There's no crying in piloting! An empty ache in my stomach turns into knots. Walking over, I awkwardly hold my arms out. She steps into them and I pat her on the back letting her cry on my shoulder.

"I'm sorry," I say, making shushing noises and wishing desperately that Jolie or Calista were here.

They would know how to help. I'm lost, holding her as she sobs. When I first met Inga she was about to be raped by those twice-damned pirates that ruined our world by wrecking our ship. We saved her from that, but she's a delicate girl. I didn't know her before, maybe she's always been this way. She doesn't deal with reality well, retreating into a protective shell.

Shidan watches with his head tilted to one side. We were speaking common so he couldn't have understood our conversation, but his empathy is apparent.

"It's fine," Inga says, taking a shaky breath. "I'm fine. We should get to work, sorry."

She wipes at the tears and I step back. I don't like being mean but I don't know how to be any different. It always sounds fine in my head but when I say things someone always gets hurt. I'm socially inept and I end up in awkward situations like this.

"You, uh, sure?" I ask Inga.

"Yes," she says, taking a deep breath. "I'm fine, promise. I was being silly I guess."

"No," I say. "It's not silly. You hope, that's what makes you you. It's a beautiful thing Inga. No matter what else, you have that. Don't let go of that."

"Okay," she smiles, her face clearing.

"Good," I say. "And who knows, maybe another big, sexy man will show up to sweep you off your feet."

She giggles, blushing hard. "You think?" she asks, her eyes darting to Shidan.

"Sure, I mean, hell, look where we are!"

"I guess that's true," she says.

"It is."

"Thank you," she says, laughing.

"Um, okay, let's get to work," I say, a tingle of pride in myself at having turned the situation around.

Going back to the motor, I remember to switch to Zmaj when I address Shidan, "You going to help or what?"

"Of course, my lyutik," he smiles. "What is it you wish?"

"Grab that thingy over there and see if it turns or not," I say, pointing at a part of the motor that looks like it should turn.

Shidan does as I ask and we all focus on the work to hand. This is better. Work I understand. It makes sense, work doesn't have emotions or feelings or get upset about things. Shidan works hard, I'll give him that. And he smells nice. There's something exotic about his scent. Almost spicy, like dark chocolate. Hmm, chocolate, damn I miss chocolate.

The most random thoughts lead back to what we've lost. Sure we're surviving and I'm grateful for it, but I miss home. I miss the camaraderie of the flight deck. I miss my old life. Living on the generation ship while we flew to some new world to colonize it. Well, my great-great grandkids or something would've colonized it. I'm not even sure, never cared. I knew my life and worked hard to get where I was.

Picking up what I think is a piston and scrubbing at the gunk on it, my mind drifts back to that first day on the flight deck.

I'M HERE. MY DREAM, MY ONE DRIVING GOAL IN LIFE RESTS ON this moment. I've done everything possible to get here, and I made it. No matter how many people said no, called me crazy, told me it couldn't be done, I did it. Walking onto the flight deck, my heart pounds in my chest like the thrumming of a Stinger's engines warming up. I can't get a deep breath, my hands shake, and tingles run up and down my spine.

The hangar is huge, forty feet to the ceiling where the cross beams criss-cross, supporting the floor above. Bright lights shine down, illuminating each of the beautiful, sleek fighters sitting in orderly rows. Mechanics run between each, servicing and making sure they're all flight ready.

The deck beneath my feet rumbles and yellow lights flash. Turning a circle, I look around in awe, trying to find the source.

"Move, idiot!" a rough, male voice yells.

The voice comes from a tall, dark-skinned man with slick, black hair who's waving his arms and yelling. My cheeks burn hot when I realize he's talking to me. I open my mouth to ask what or where when the rumbling beneath my feet increase and it hits me. I'm on a landing strip! Glancing over my shoulder, I see running lights that lead to an open bay door and the force shield that holds the vacuum of space at bay. A small dot moves closer, then I see blue flame behind it.

Bursting into motion, I run towards the man who's still yelling. The rumble is vibrating up through my feet making my knees ache. Reaching the yelling man he grabs my arm and jerks me forward. Behind me there's a rush of air and the rumbling slows and stops.

"The hell is wrong with you?" the man asks, not letting go of my arm and jerking me around to face him.

I can't help but notice the sergeant stripes on his shoulder.

"Sorry sir," I say, mouth so dry I can barely force words out.

"Sir?" he barks. "I work for a living, Pilot!"

"Yes, sergeant," I say, abashed, but despite embarrassment pride swells my chest. He called me Pilot.

"You are greener than anything I've ever seen," he mutters. "Let me see your orders."

Holding my pad screen out, he takes it and swipes a finger across. He reads page after page of my orders and apparently my entire personnel file, and while he does, everyone on deck seems to stare at me. Whether that's because of my ineptitude at standing at the end of a launch tube while a fighter was landing or because I'm the first woman they've ever seen in this area is unclear.

"Stancher," he mutters, glancing up at me then back down at the pad screen.

"Yes, sergeant," I agree, acknowledging my name because I don't know what else to say.

He shakes his head, bites his lower lip then looks at me again. "Of all the hair-brained ideas," he says, looking me up and down with a critical eye. "You know you don't belong here right?"

"No sergeant," I say, snapping to attention. "I do not."

"By all that's holy, what the hell is wrong with you Pilot?"

"Nothing, sergeant," I snap. "I'm a Pilot. This is where I belong."

A snicker rises from the men behind him. His head swivels like a gun on a turret searching for a target. All the men behind him become very busy or do their best to appear so.

"This ain't no Battlestar Galactica, Stancher," he snaps, attention fully back on me. "And you sure as hell ain't no Starbuck."

"No sergeant," I answer.

"You earn your place."

"Yes, sergeant."

"Well enough, your scores are high but we'll see how that translates in the big black won't we? I don't want to be scraping no damn Stancher off the side of my beautiful ship, do you understand me?"

"Yes sergeant."

He nods then storms away without another word. Watching his retreat, my stomach twists and turns. Inhaling a slow, shaky breath, I move out of full standing at full attention. This isn't the welcome I expected at all. Where's the camaraderie among those who risk their lives every day to keep the ship safe from threats? Turning a slow circle, I'm lost and I'm alone. The first woman to make it past the rigorous training regime and graduate flight school. Now I'm here but there's no welcoming committee.

"Hey," a man says, walking up and holding out his hand. "Welcome to the flight deck."

He has an easy, welcoming grin that lights up his tanned face. Taking his hand I shake it firmly and nod.

"Thanks."

"Don't worry about the Sarge," he says, nodding his head back towards the sergeant's retreating figure. "He's always like that."

"I'm Draker, you must be Stancher," he says crossing his arms over his chest.

"Yeah," I say. "Guess everyone heard the sergeant."

"Hell, we didn't need his show to know who you are, your reputation proceeds you."

Three more guys walk up and join us, one of them is wearing flight leathers that creak as he approaches.

"Who's the grub trying to block my landing bare-handed?" the one in flight leathers asks.

"This is Stancher," Draker says.

"No shit?" the other three say in unison.

"Well, welcome to flight deck," flight leathers says. "I'm Apollo but you can call me Ben."

Ben grins. Instantly I like him. Draker looks between the two of us then shakes his head.

"This is Jackson, and that there is Tomas, he's just an engineer, so nothing important," Draker says, and I can't tell if he's serious or not.

"Hey," Tomas says.

"Hi," I greet them all. This is more like what I expected.

"So is it true?" Ben asks, looking at me inquisitively.

"Is what true?"

"That you got a perfect score on the flight sim?"

All four guys lean in like they're expecting to hear some big secret. My cheeks burn and my mouth goes dry. Looking at the floor I shrug. Bragging gets you nowhere my mom used to say.

"No way," Tomas breathes.

11

I shrug again then meet Ben's eyes. Respect shines out of them.

"You're my new flight partner," he says, grinning.

"Hey," Draker exclaims.

"What?" Ben asks.

The mood changes to tense fast but it doesn't seem to bother Ben.

"Come on Stancher," he says, putting an arm around my shoulders. I stiffen at the unwelcome attention but he pulls me along. "We're going to see the Lieutenant."

Glancing over my shoulder, Draker glares at the two of us as we walk away.

SNORTING, I SHAKE MY HEAD TO CLEAR IT OF MEMORIES. BEING a female pilot, I had to work twice as hard, do twice as much as any of the guys to prove myself. Girls weren't pilots, everyone knew that. That's what they said. When I enlisted and applied, they tried every way in the world to keep me out. It didn't matter because I was ready for that. I knew what I wanted and I would have it.

Except it's all gone. What I told Inga is true too. It's over and I'll never have it back. Now I'm a half-ass engineer working on alien technology I wouldn't understand even if I was a real engineer. If this was a Stinger, we'd all be in business. I always worked on my Stinger along with Tomas, the flight engineer assigned to my ship. If you want to know your ship, take it apart and put it back together. When you know every single nut and bolt then you know a ship, Tomas used to say. I agreed with him.

But none of that translates to getting this city's power grid working. That I've got it working at all is more of a miracle than I want everyone to know. They're counting on me and I'm the best we've got. Which isn't saying much.

"Can you lift this?" I ask Shidan, pointing at the massive motor in front of me.

"Of course," he smiles, flexing his arms and rolling his shoulders.

Rolling my eyes, I step back. He bends his knees and grabs the bottom side of the generator. Muscles ripple and flex as he straightens, giving only the slightest of grunts. Damn if he isn't strong. And sexy. No, damn it, he's not sexy, he's an annoying alien who stares at me with fiery eyes that smolder too much to be puppy dog eyes.

Stop it Amara! I'm no one's treasure, and that's all he wants. A Zmaj doesn't understand how to treat a woman as an equal. I've seen it with my friends. Over-protective and jealous. He's not for me. Besides, I know better than to let anyone else close.

"Thanks," I say, kneeling and reaching under to adjust the gauge I hope will increase the power output.

"Of course my lyutik," he replies.

He always calls me that. I don't know what it means as it doesn't seem to translate into Common. I'm sure it's some misogynistic term meaning I'm his treasure or some crap. I'm not a flower, damn it.

Once the gauge turns I slide clear. "Clear," I say, and Shidan lowers the motor to the ground.

His biceps flex and ripple as he does. He turns his head towards me, a grin on his face. I'm strangely aware of my heart beating, rapid, like it's thrumming. No, no, no. Get it under control Amara, what the hell is wrong with you?

"Why do you call me that?" I snap, desperate to distract myself.

He tilts his head to one side. "What?" he asks, like he doesn't have a clue.

"Lyutik," I repeat it slowly, the word strange on my tongue.

He smiles and shrugs instead of answering.

"Well quit it."

"As you wish." Shidan grins again before turning his back on me.

Inga chuckles from where she's working and I sigh, climbing to my feet to inspect the machine. It's still humming softly but the gauge I think shows the output hasn't changed.

"Damn it," I mutter.

"You will figure it out," Shidan insists.

"Sure," I agree half-heartedly.

I take a seat on an old crate and stare. Shidan stands to my left quietly watching. The sound of the motor's humming and Inga cleaning parts is soothing. I let my eyes wander over the machines, hoping for inspiration.

"I must go to my patrol," Shidan says, breaking into my musing.

"Oh, sure," I say.

Sverre spotted a ship full of space pirates a while back and we've kept regular patrols of the city perimeter since. The space pirates brought down our ship, and it turns out they're slavers with a long, unfriendly history with the Zmaj. Definitely not the kind of people you invite over for dinner.

"I will see you tomorrow," he says, waving as he leaves.

I watch him go and the room seems emptier without him in it.

"You two should go on a date," Inga says once he's gone.

"A date? Seriously? And do what? It's not like we have any movies to go to or someplace to go out to dinner."

"That just means it cuts down on the in-between. Skip the boring and go straight to the good stuff," she grins and I roll my eyes.

"I don't have alien baby fever," I respond, and she laughs.

Footsteps clang musically on the metal stairs leading to

the sub-basement. Inga and I jump, turning towards the sound. Mei glides into view, moving in a hurry.

"What's up Mei?"

"Calista's in trouble, we need you," she exhales.

"What kind of trouble?" Inga asks before I can.

"The baby."

Shit. Am I supposed to be a doctor now, too? The other two women look at me like a bunch of green pilots unsure how to fasten their safety harnesses.

"All right, let's go," I order, rushing past Mei and leading the way up the stairs.

I don't know what I can do but I guess I'll figure that out when I get there.

2

SHIDAN

"No Shidan, you do not understand," Sverre says.

We're walking the perimeter of the dome that covers and protects the city. The air is too cool for my taste but the humans do not deal well with the heat outside even after taking the life-giving epis plant. Their bodies aren't designed for the climate of Tajss. The dome sparkles in the light of the double red suns and gives the view outside an odd hue. It's pretty. I barely remember the domes that covered our cities before the devastation.

"But why?" I ask.

It's so confusing. Amara is perfect, beautiful, all I want is to treasure her. Care for her forever but she rejects me at every turn. I do not understand these human females.

Sverre sighs. "This I do not know," he says, holding his hands up before him. "It is their nature. Perhaps it is because of their home world. The human females want to feel equal to their mate."

"This makes no sense!" I exclaim, my voice rising with frustration.

Sverre hisses, a low, dangerous sound. My tail stiffens as

instinct kicks in, preparing for him to attack. Sverre turns towards me and his wings shudder as he struggles. Red tints his eyes and the edges of his scales darken. His frown deepens, he's bigger than I am, a much more experienced warrior, and my elder. I step back, giving deference but not dropping my guard. My scales itch and I hold my breath waiting.

Sverre takes a deep breath then exhales a soft hiss. Shaking his head, he glares at me. "You should know better," he says.

"Apologies, Councilor." I bow my head.

"Accepted. The bijass is strong, we must be careful in our interactions. Do not press the others, many would not have hesitated so long to destroy you."

They would try, I think, but I smile and nod my agreement.

There's no reason to antagonize him. The bijass is strong and I feel it too. After the devastation, when there was but a handful of our race left and I among the youngest that survived, it started. Some kind of regression to our more primal instincts. It made us territorial and unable to trust each other. Our memories faded, becoming dim and distant. Life before the devastation isn't something I remember, but it doesn't matter. What I remember of life before was not a life worth living. I had no mate, no one to share my joy with.

All I've come through is the trials necessary to bring me to Amara. The call of her is a twisting in my core, an empty ache, a need to have her. She is my treasure. I knew it the first moment I saw her. We are meant to be together. Every fiber of my being calls to her.

"Still," I say, keeping my emotions under control. "It makes little sense. She is not my equal, she is far greater. A treasure to be worshiped. How can she not know this?"

"I understand Shidan but they are not Zmaj," he shakes his head. "Until you grasp that difference you will not gain understanding."

The confusion whirls in my soul like a black pit left behind by the zemlja, one of the great sand worm that tunnel their way beneath the surface of Tajss.

"These females are too complex!" I shout at nothing and no one.

Sverre nods his agreement. "But," he holds up a finger and his tail sways faster. "That makes them a worthy treasure. Would you want a treasure you did not have to earn?"

I think about that as we walk. His words are true and wise. As they should be, he's an Elder and a Councilor. Amara awakens something deep inside me I cannot put into words. Thoughts, feelings, and a longing need. She is perfect, amazing, the lines of her jaw are strong and imperious. The other females wear the fur on their heads longer but not my Amara. She keeps hers cut short, close to her head. There's a practicality to this I'm sure, but it makes her beautiful, letting the lines of her face and neck shine without distraction.

"I'm sure you are right," I say.

"I am," he agrees. "You are young. Did you ever have a mate?"

"No, I did not."

"I see," he says. "So the desires are new to you."

"I knew about them!" I say, defensively.

"Ah, yes you did, but after the devastation everything changed. The desires, our instinct to have and protect a mate, are stronger and harder to resist."

"Yes," I agree.

This I know well. The drive to be near her, to protect her is all-consuming. Her resistance does nothing to abate it. No matter how she acts I must be near her. It's the only thing that calms the need. Even now, being away from her makes my scales itch like something deep inside my brain I can't reach. I can't stop it. Part of my thoughts are on her, always. It's strange, wonderful, and distracting all at the same time.

Something flashes in the distance. I notice but wouldn't have given it a second thought if Sverre did not stop and turn. His second lids shut, filtering the light, but even so he shields his eyes with his hands. Jerked out of my own thoughts, my scales tingle, alert as my senses go into over-drive. Danger? My stomach tightens as anger flashes red hot, ready to destroy anything or anyone that would dare to threaten Amara, my lyutik.

"Is it…" I don't finish the thought.

It's unnecessary to say the word. We don't patrol the city perimeter for entertainment. The dome is more than suffi-cient to keep out natural threats but we have to worry about Zzlo. Zzlo are slavers. When I was a child, they were the monster that parents used to scare children. They would get any petulant Zmaj child to go to bed or behave with the threat they would steal you away and sell you off-world. I've never seen one myself, but Sverre ran across them recently.

Fantasies come to life. Before the devastation there were always rumors of them having kidnapped workers. It might have been true too. They never came near the cities though and that's where I grew up. It was always some outpost or a group of gatherers getting epis who didn't come back.

Now we are not prepared to fight them if they come in force. Listening to Amara talk, I can guess that the Zzlo were the ones who attacked her ship. I guess I should be grateful to them for bringing her but they are undeserving. They will get nothing from me but death.

"No," Sverre says at last and I feel him relax. "How is the work coming to bring the power up to full status?"

"Good," I lie. Amara is doing the best she can. There is no point in creating more stress for her.

"Good, we need to bring the defenses on line," he mutters as we resume our patrol.

"We should find them and attack them."

"And what good would that do?"

"Surprise, if we surprise them then we can drive them off our planet."

"Yes," he nods. "That would work perhaps for this crew of them. What about the next?"

"What next? We'll destroy all that come at us. I won't let anyone threaten her!"

My ire rises, my tail stiffening as my wings open and my fists ball.

Sverre smiles. I wrestle with an instinct to punch him and destroy that smile. Its deep and strong, a pulsing desire to beat him down, force him to his knees.

"Shidan, believe me, they are numerous. If you see a ship of them, which I have, it is but an expedition force. We do not have the numbers to take them on."

"We have to protect them," I say, meaning Amara and he knows it.

"You will," he says. "Just as I must Jolie. We will. That, more than anything else, gives us the strength to resist the bijass."

It does nothing to satisfy my anger but I accept his response. My scales burn at the edges as I struggle to contain my rage. There is no target for it I can do anything about. An impending threat to Amara's safety I can do nothing to stop. We walk in silence until the anger fades away at last, the red mist of the bijass loosening its grip on the edges of my thoughts.

"I wish I understood these humans better," I observe. "Why does she not want me to do things for her? She differs from how Jolie is with you or Calista with Ladon."

"This is true," Sverre says. "Though I do not know why it is."

"Maybe Jolie can explain."

"Perhaps," Sverre says. "It is worth asking."

"I will do that tonight," I say. Having a direction is satisfying at least.

We finish our patrol in silence. The city is huge and we walk its entire perimeter looking for anything that seems out of place or signs of trouble. It's boring work but necessary. When we finish, Sverre and I go to his home. As we enter the dim, cool building my wings rustle and the edges of my scales color light blue. It's too cool in here. The humans like it so I tolerate it but I prefer to be outside in the warmth.

Entering their apartment Jolie approaches us. Her dark hair is shoulder length framing delicate features. Her eyes vary from the other females and her skin has a gold tint. She's tiny, too breakable in my mind, unlike Amara who has nice strong curves on her hips and incredible mounds under her blouse. The bulge of Jolie's stomach sticks out so far I wonder how she walks, but I've figured out enough to know not to ask. Apparently this is a bad topic with the human females.

She's upset. It fills the room with an oppressiveness that makes it hard to breathe. Her eyes are puffy, cheeks blotchy, and there are hints of moisture in her eyes. Sverre crosses the room in a flurry of motion, wrapping his arms protectively around her. She wraps her own around him and lays her head on his chest. My stomach burns watching them. What I would give for Amara to be in my arms. He enfolds her, protects her from the world, takes her cares away.

"What has happened?" Sverre asks.

"Nothing, I'm just... I'm happy you're home," she says.

Sverre leans close and murmurs words I can't hear. Feeling awkward I turn and face the door to give them privacy. After a time Sverre clears his throat and I turn back.

"Is everything okay?" I ask.

Sverre looks at Jolie who shrugs.

"Calista might have complications with her pregnancy," she says.

"Might?"

Calista is Ladon's treasure. They were the first pairing of humans and Zmaj and while Jolie is also pregnant, Calista is further along. The compatibility of our two races was unexpected so everyone in the community, human and Zmaj alike, have a great interest in her well-being.

"There were difficulties," Jolie says.

"Is she fine?" I ask.

"Yes, we think so," Jolie says. "No one is sure, we don't have the equipment to do much of an exam and no one is an actual baby doctor."

A cold chill races between my wings and down my tail. She has to be fine. If she's not, then that means our races aren't compatible. What chance will I stand with Amara if that is the case?

"Is there anything we can do?" I ask.

Jolie shrugs. There's something about her I can't put my finger on, a weight on her shoulders and a sunken look to her eyes. I'm used to her being a happy, vibrant person but tonight she seems distracted and sad. Watching her movements I follow her hands then my eyes land on her belly. Of course! She's worried for her own child.

"No," she replies.

"Perhaps we should continue our work another time," I offer.

"No, please, it gives me something to focus on."

"If you're certain."

She smiles and I see a glimmer of the Jolie I know in her eyes. "I'm certain," she says, motioning towards the seats. I take one and she sits opposite me. "Now, where did we leave off?"

"You were explaining how some words have more than one meaning," I say.

"Ah, yes," she smiles. Jolie tries to explain this most confusing part of her language. I do my best to follow along but it's difficult. The concept is strange. Why could they not come up with a new word for new things? Why twist one word to mean many things? Another mystery of the humans. We speak Common so I can try to learn.

"How are things with the two of you?" she asks after a while, switching back to the Zmaj language.

"The same," I say. "She pushes me away."

"Are you… sure?"

"Sure?"

"Yeah, that, well I mean… Amara is, well she can be… abrasive."

She's being careful with what she says which I appreciate but I know what she means. Jolie is Amara's friend yes, but Amara isn't always nice. I don't think she means to be mean though. She says what's on her mind.

"She is perfect," I reply.

"Sure," Jolie says. "If you like that kind of thing."

Tilting my head to one side I stare. I don't understand her reference.

Jolie shakes her head and shrugs. "She's controlling," she continues. "And dominating and well, in all honesty she can be a bitch."

"A bitch?" I ask confused. "This is not a Zmaj word."

Jolie's cheeks flush a bright red. Her mouth moves but no words come out. She holds her hand up in front of herself and waves them. I sit and wait, feeling lost.

"It's a, not nice word. It means a female dog, but it also means a woman who is being… not nice."

"Ah," I say, thinking about this. "So if you were being mean to Sverre, you would be a bitch?"

23

Her eyes widen and her mouth forms an O. "Um, well, yeah, I guess so."

"Bitch," I say, rolling the word around on my tongue. It has an interesting feel to it when I say it. "So Rosalind is a bitch?"

"Oh lord," Jolie says. "Um, look, that's not a good word and I sure wouldn't use it regarding the Lady General, especially if she can hear you."

"I don't understand," I say, tilting my head again.

"There are words we consider being… not nice. Impolite. You shouldn't use them around others."

"Then why do you have these words?"

"Because…" she trails off.

"You have words that mean things then someone decides some of these words aren't nice. They aren't nice but they're still there?"

"Pretty much," she says.

"Humans are strange."

"Yeah, I guess we are," she agrees.

"Are there many of these word?"

"Yeah, quite a few. We call them curse words."

"Curse words? So they bring bad luck to the target?"

"Well no, but sort of. I mean they'll start a fight because people get offended by them."

"This makes no sense," I observe.

"Yeah, well, welcome to the Common tongue," she laughs. "It's just one of the many mysteries of our race. So, moving on, are things getting better with her?"

"I do not know," I answer honestly.

Jolie smiles, pats my hand then leans back in the chair resting her hands on her growing stomach. She looks tired.

"It is late, I should leave."

She smiles but doesn't argue. I've overstayed my welcome in her home.

"Have a good night," she says.

"You too."

I make my farewells before heading to the small building I call home.

I have much to think about. The human language is complex and many of its sounds are hard to produce with my mouth but I'm learning. Once I'm proficient, I will tell Amara how much she means in her own tongue.

I will win her. She will be mine, forever.

3

AMARA

"*S*o go over the situation with me again, from the top," Rosalind says.

I sigh. Rosalind is the de facto leader of the humans. She's beautiful, with long dark hair and haughty, imperial features. She's in control and you know it the moment she walks in. On the ship she was the Lady General and even I, having been a female pilot, can only imagine what it took for her to earn and keep that position. She's never bitchy even if she comes across as cold. Her white suit creaks as she moves. It's a subtle sound but I recognize it from my flight suits. It's made of the same material. Clever.

We're in an old building that has a lot of floors and is still mostly intact. It's used as a meeting place and the Council gathers around a table, comprised of eight humans plus Sverre, Jolie's mate, and Ladon, Calista's mate representing the Zmaj. Only fair since before we showed up Ladon had the entire city to himself.

Zmaj struggle with a primal part of them which makes them want to kill each other on sight, so for the benefit of everyone we avoid having too many in a room at the same time. The humans are my friends, mostly, Rosalind, Jolie, Mei, Calista are in that category. Then there are a few who represent the other 'interest' group, the Humanist as they call themselves. I call them backwards thinking xenophobes.

Rosalind watches patiently, waiting for me to start again. She has that skill which I've never mastered. Patience. Bane of my existence.

Ladon drums the table with his fingers, his wings flutter, and his tail is switching back and forth. There's no hiding his agitation and concern. Ladon is big, even for a Zmaj. His scales are tan with yellow and blue accents at the edges. I wonder if the colors mean something.

"The long and short of it is, we don't know," I say. "We need machines. Better yet, we need a doctor, one who's familiar with both Zmaj and Human biology if we're throwing our wishes at the stars."

Rosalind nods.

"What else did you expect?" Gershom pipes in.

Gershom, damn I hate him. A walking douche bag if ever there was one. Loud, brash, full of himself and now he's come out as a racist dick to top it all off. What blows my mind is he has followers among the survivors. Other humans who think we should isolate ourselves from the Zmaj. Ones who aren't happy with the choices some of the girls have made about who to invite to their bed.

I'd say it was all some kind of male chauvinist thing, but there are women among his followers. He's always striving against Rosalind, pushing the boundaries and vying for power. Which is what I think he really wants. I suspect that all the rhetoric is smoke and mirrors. Power is the real goal. Power for himself so he can always get his own way. He's a tool, a class-A tool.

"What do you mean Gershom?" Rosalind asks, like anyone here doesn't know what he meant.

"There has been a rash of bad... choices," he pauses, long enough for everyone to read into the blank what he means. "As far as we know we are the only survivors of the world ship, we have a duty and an obligation to our race and our ancestors. We may not have made it to our destination planet, but fate has chosen this one for us."

"Fate?" Rosalind says, derision clear in the tone of her voice. "Seriously Gershom?"

"Mock me if you must Rosalind," he says and a soft murmur comes from his supporters at the table.

I don't know their names, don't care either. They're ridiculous to the point of bordering on insane. I don't like them, want nothing to do with them, and would prefer they not be here.

"I'm not mocking you Gershom," Rosalind says with an even tone. "I question your viewpoint."

Gershom smiles and shakes his head. "Of course you do," he says with so much condescension my skin crawls.

"Make your point Gershom."

"My point is," he says, "the ones having— difficulty, have earned their due. It in no way should hinder or endanger the rest of the survivors."

"Noted," Rosalind says.

Ladon's wings rustle, opening and closing, then he rises to his feet and leans over, placing his elbows on the table and staring directly at me.

"What kind of machine is it you need?" he asks.

"Can someone translate what this monster just said?" Gershom asks.

Ladon turns his head and hisses, his wings spreading as his hands ball into fists. Gershom slides his chair back and it falls over. He leaps to his feet stumbling backwards. His hands flail ineffectively in front of himself as he struggles to maintain his balance. I don't bother trying to hide my amusement. I'm not the only one to laugh out loud.

Gershom and his Humanists have refused to learn the Zmaj language, which is as easy as standing in front of one of the few working machines on the planet and having it placed in your head. Since we humans don't have a machine that teaches the Zmaj Common, it's a one way flow. They don't get to learn ours in return.

"See!" Gershom exclaims.

"See what? You bumbling around like an idiot?" I ask.

He and his supporters glare at me like I've grown a second head. I grin, welcoming their dislike since it's mutual. Rosalind sighs and translates for Gershom, while Sverre and Ladon watch the humans work out their own issues. Ladon stands up, crossing his arms across his massive chest. His arms are like big logs, bulging muscles and manliness. He glares at Gershom without saying a word.

"Something that will let us see inside of Calista," I say. "We call them ultrasound machines."

Ladon and Sverre exchange looks then Sverre shrugs.

"Ultrasound?" Ladon asks.

"Yeah, it uses sound waves to construct a picture of what's going on inside. We don't know how… hmmm," I trail off trying to find words for what I want to say without being too blunt.

"Know what?" Ladon hisses.

"Well, to be blunt, what your baby is doing to Calista's insides. I wouldn't have guessed that cross-species impregnation was possible."

"I see," Ladon mumbles. His shoulders slump as his wings close tight and his tail drops to the ground.

"We had medical facilities," Sverre says. "Perhaps they are still working?"

Of course? Why hadn't I thought of that? The Zmaj had

all kinds of cool tech back in the day. It seems obvious they would have had decent medical care too.

"Worth a shot," I say.

As I talk with Ladon and Sverre another girl translates for Gershom and his close-minded morons.

"Prioritization of any facilities or resources should be for human needs first," Gershom says, slamming a fist down on the table.

"What do you think we're talking about? Calista and Jolie are both human!" I shout, glaring at the translator. Quit being helpful, then we can just tell Gershom whatever we think he can handle. Ugh.

"No, they're not! They have slept with these… things. Their decisions may cost them their lives but that's on them. There are plenty of surviving humans. They could contribute to our society instead of spawning… whatever they will be having."

He bites off the words he wants to say and I see it clear as day. I know what he wanted to say. Anger flashes white hot.

"You small-minded, ignorant, self-centered, worthless bastard," I rise to my feet. "How is your head so far up your own ass?"

"What are you talking about?" he asks.

"You're a racist," I declare.

"No, I'm not," he says defensively. "Anything but."

"So what if you have transferred your ignorance to the aliens instead of singling out a different skin color? I've studied the documentaries. I know what Earth was like when we left."

"I'm doing no such thing," he says. "I'm planning for the survival of our race."

"You're impossible."

The men with him move closer. I want to jump across the table and slap that knowing smirk off his face. My pulse pounds in my ears. Digging my nails into my palms I struggle to control the anger. It won't do any good. I sit back in my chair, closing my eyes and shaking my head.

"Where is this equipment?" Rosalind asks, bring the conversation back to the point at hand.

"I can lead the way," Ladon says.

"I'll go," I say.

Rosalind nods then adjourns the meeting. I sit and watch everyone filing out until it's just Rosalind, Ladon and I.

"Why do you put up with him?" I ask.

"Because he has a right to his thoughts," Rosalind says. "If we lose that, then we lose everything that makes us human."

"But he's a monster!"

"No, he's not. An instigator? Yes. A scared, little man who's afraid that he will die alone? Probably. That doesn't change that he has a right to feel like he feels."

"He's gathering followers," I say.

"I know," Rosalind says, implacable.

"Okay, well he's a douche and I can't stand him."

Rosalind smiles. "I know."

"Good," I say, looking up at Ladon. "Shall we go?"

"Yes."

We walk out of the Council chambers and Shidan is waiting right outside the door. Ladon hisses at the unexpected presence and the two of them glare at each other. Shidan is smaller than Ladon but doesn't back down. It's admirable and a random, primal part of me feels excited but I push that aside.

"What are you doing here?" I ask, doing my best to defuse the situation before anything escalates.

I've had two Zmaj fighting over me. It's a sexy idea for a story but in reality it's scary as hell and not sexy at all.

"I am here for you, my lyutik," Shidan says.

Ladon glances between the two of us when Shidan says

the word that doesn't seem to translate. My cheeks flush hotly. I know the word means more than I think it does and it's driving me nuts, but no one I've asked knows what it means. Or if they do, they're not telling.

"Why?" I ask.

Shidan smiles and shrugs.

I roll my eyes. "You're like the stray cat that once you feed it, it won't go away."

"A cat? What is a cat?" Ladon asks.

"Never mind," I shake my head. "Let's go look at this equipment of yours."

Ladon takes off and I follow behind, Shidan falling in next to me. The sun's glare through the dome reflects off the ruined buildings. Waves of heat rise from the cracked, over-grown streets. Everything is quiet. My entire life before the crash was on the ship. It was 'normal' but it was still a ship. Tight quarters, limited space, but filled with life. I was never alone. We even shared quarters. It was nothing like walking around this dead, empty world.

I hate to admit it but I'm glad to have Shidan by my side. I wouldn't think it would bother me. My favorite thing about being a pilot was to get off the ship out into the big black. The quiet and solitude while flying my fighter was a welcome escape from daily life. But the city is too quiet. There are too many places for things to hide. Space is open, you know what's out there as far as the eye can see. There're no corners or shadows for things to hide in and jump out at you. Oh and nothing is looking to eat you, unlike here. It makes my skin crawl thinking about it.

Shidan walks with a swagger that calms my nerves. He's certain, shows no fear, the world has nothing that scares him. At least that's the way he seems. It's nice. So there's at least one reason to keep him around. Even though he's annoying. If he'd just quit trying to do everything for me maybe he'd be better. I shake my head and push aside thoughts like that. I don't need anyone, I know what happens if I let someone close. I won't let it happen again. Besides, everyone is depending on me to do a job I don't know how to do. I got enough on my plate.

"How much farther?" I ask, my throat dry and scratchy.

I didn't think to bring any water with me. I assumed our destination wouldn't be that far since it's inside the dome but it's still hot, too hot. Stupid hot, to the point you can fry your food on the streets.

"We are almost there," Ladon says without looking back.

"Are you okay, my lyutik?" Shidan asks, concern obvious in his voice.

"I'm fine," I snap.

A quick dart of his eyes to the ground is the only sign of the hurt my words inflict. Why did I do that? I didn't have to, he was being nice. Agh, why am I letting him get under my skin? I don't have time for this. Besides, I'm not his damn treasure! I'm not a porcelain doll that might break at the slightest breeze. I'm as tough as anyone and I don't need taking care of.

"Of course," he says, smiling.

If only he knew, I'm doing it for his own good.

"Here," Ladon says, saving me from having to figure out how to deal with the situation.

"Damn," I exhale, looking at the building. "Did a bomb go off?"

The front looks like an explosion happened. Steel girders bend and twist like some giant hand molded them into abstract art. Scattered debris litters the opening and is strewn out across the street.

"Perhaps," Ladon says, picking a path through the mess.

I exchange a rueful glance with Shidan before following. Rusted cable hangs loose from the ceiling and the walls.

33

Broken machines lie across the floor mixed among the debris. Ladon works his way to a door which hangs ajar on its hinges at the rear of what once might have been a lobby.

Reaching the door, my stomach clenches tight as I see bite marks on the door frame. Bite marks. Shit are there monsters in here with us? Ladon sees, touching them with his finger tips, then moves past like it means nothing. Goosebumps race down my arms and a chill goes along my spine. Swallowing hard, I follow behind, unwilling to show fear.

The light from outside is dim. Shadows encroach on what little illumination passes the door and beyond it is pitch blackness. Something shifts then falls and I jump with a yelp. Shidan whirls, dropping into a crouch at the same time pushing me behind him with one arm. He moves faster than I can regain my senses. Ladon crouches in a similar stance, both men waiting for an attack.

My palms itch for my control stick. My finger twitches, ready to pull the trigger that will unleash a hail of death from my weapons, none of which I have. I'm not in my fighter, I'm unarmed and dependent. My skin crawls as I realize, perhaps for the first time, how vulnerable I truly am. My stomach fills with acid then clenches tight, forcing the burning liquid up my throat. Something moves, shifting in the shadows. Ladon holds up two fingers them moves them back and forth. Shidan nods and Ladon steps out, one, then two. The darkness closes around him until he's a shadowy figure himself.

Quiet. There's not a sound except for my heart beating so loud that it's making my head pound. I don't breathe. I don't dare. Something is out there in the darkness. Shidan's wings rustle, breaking the heavy silence with their soft, leathery sound. His tail brushes against my leg and I suppress a yelp.

Something crashes and I can't suppress that yelp.

Ladon lands on his back in the streaming light. Something is on top of him. I can't tell what it is.

There are teeth, lots of snapping, sharp teeth and drool falling in Ladon's face. Deafening noise fills the blackness as they slam together, over and over. Ladon struggles with it, barely holding it from shredding his face.

Shidan attacks, punching past the light. The blow lands on something solid, a thud echoing through the space. Shidan swings his tail around and slams it down on top of the monster. Grabbing the nearest thing to hand, I swing two-handed without thinking, slamming it against the creature. There's a satisfying thunk as I connect, then vibrations run up my arms, numbing them.

The thing screeches, a high-pitched sound that scrapes across my nerves like nails on a chalkboard.

Ladon pushes up, his tail swinging, smashing into the monster. Shidan spreads his wings and leaps into the air, slamming down into the creature and something snaps. It drops with a thud and then there's silence. Ladon pushes the thing off of him, its claws and teeth scraping across the ruined floor.

My heart is pounding, my chest hurts, it's hard to breathe. Air comes in ragged gasps. My hands are shaking and a shudder runs along my back.

"Are you okay?" Shidan asks, grasping my shoulders.

"What the hell was that?" I ask, looking up into his warm, yellow eyes.

Shidan shrugs, looking over at. "Looks like a guster, big one. Must have been stuck in here since you got the dome working."

"Just… damn."

He nods before turning and offering a hand to Ladon.

"Thank you," Ladon says, climbing to his feet.

"I hate this place," I exhale, still trying to calm my nerves.

They look at me like I'm the one who's nuts. It may be normal for them but I'm not used to being attacked by every damn thing coming out of the shadows. It's not right. Ladon digs into a pack on his side and pulls out a torch, lighting it with a puff of flame from his mouth. That weirds me out. Fire-breathing dragon men is just strange. How does kissing work with that?

Glancing at Shidan, an urge to find out grips me. I bet his lips would taste great with that exotic spicy chocolate odor he puts off— no, Amara. No. You know you can't do that. I can't let him in.

Ladon waves his torch around, pushing back the shadows. The flickering light makes my stomach sink, pushing away any last vestiges of burgeoning desires. The place is wrecked. There's nothing useful here. Whatever that thing was, it looks like it tried to eat everything in the room. All the equipment has visible bite marks. Metal containers with chunks ripped from it by teeth.

"Are we sure that thing is dead?" I ask, looking at the damage it caused.

Both men look over their shoulders at the dead body.

"Yes," Shidan answers.

"Well good but so is all this equipment," I sigh, poking through the machines. "This is a bust."

4

SHIDAN

"*T*o put it as bluntly as possible, we are one hundred percent screwed," Amara says.

Rosalind nods and Ladon paces, his long strides carrying him back and forth across the room in three steps. The human known as Gershom smiles and has a smug look on his face. He makes my scales itch. An urge to toss him out the window grips me but I have to resist. It wouldn't be right no matter how much he deserves it. He's rude and mean to my lyutik. It would bring me great pleasure to show him the error of his ways. I exercise restraint mostly because I don't want Amara to know I understand what he's saying. I'm not ready yet for her to know I am learning her language.

"We have to help her," Ladon hisses, crossing his arms over his chest.

His agitation is apparent in his stance, motion and the red-green tint to the edges of his scales. I understand. His control is admirable. If Amara was in as much danger as his treasure, I wouldn't be as in control of myself.

"What are our options?" Rosalind asks, looking at Amara.

Amara frowns, her brow furrowing together. Her lips

purse making my core tighten, what I would give to taste those sweet lips!

"We don't have many. My one hope right now is to increase the power flow through the city. Jolie found a box outside the dome," Amara says. "I went to investigate it a few months ago but then Shidan and Astarot showed up. I haven't gone back to it. I've been busy trying to get the motors inside the dome working."

"So what are you suggesting?" Rosalind asks.

"I go check it out. There's too much we don't know. Maybe it has a buried line running somewhere, maybe it's a power booster, or maybe it's a key to something else. If we can open it up, I can figure out what it's for, I think."

"That's a lot of maybes," Rosalind observes.

"Common, please!" Gershom interjects, slapping his hand on the table making a loud sound.

My scales crawl at the sound of his voice. I walk over to stand behind where he's sitting and lean in so I'm looming over him. Just enough to make him nervous. He shifts in his seat. Amara smiles and my hearts leap in my chest, pounding so hard I wonder that no one in the room can hear.

Rosalind translates for Gershom but I notice she doesn't give him all the details, just a brief version. He doesn't complain and seems satisfied, which amuses me. He crouches further down in his chair as I continue my game of looming above him.

"Can someone move their pet monster?"

"Move him yourself," Amara says.

Gershom's entire body shakes then, bracing himself, he turns on his seat to face me. He places both hands against my chest and pushes. His strength is negligible and does nothing. I look down at him and tilt my head.

"Is there an issue?" I ask in Zmaj, smiling.

"What is this thing saying?"

"He says he wants to eat you," Amara snaps.

I mustn't laugh! She can't know that I understand her.

"Amara!" Rosalind chides. "He asked if there's something wrong, Gershom."

"There is! He's looming over me. Haven't these walking beasts heard of personal space?" Gershom says.

Amara laughs and my hearts sing. Rosalind glares at me and it's clear she knows I'm doing this on purpose. I don't care. Amara's laughter makes it all worth it.

"Shidan, leave the human alone," Ladon says.

The pain and upset in his voice takes the fun out of my game. Glancing at Amara, I step away from Gershom.

"I don't like you going outside the dome Amara, you're too valuable. You're the closest thing to an engineer we have."

"Which is why it has to be me that goes," she replies.

Rosalind stares into the distance before giving a sharp nod. "You're right, we have no choice."

"I will go with her," I say.

Rosalind turns. Her eyes look deep into me, judging, until she seems to find me worthy. She gives the same sharp nod.

"What is this?" Gershom asks. "What's going on? We haven't voted on anything!"

"Amara is going outside the dome to investigate the box. We need to see if and how it ties into the city systems."

"And I suppose one of these aliens is going with her?" Gershom asks.

"Yes," Rosalind says.

"I want a human with them," he says.

"Amara is human," Rosalind points out.

Gershom glances at her sidelong. "I don't trust these aliens, I want someone with them that has a more... open viewpoint."

"Are you kidding me?" Amara rises from her seat, her face

flushing a bright red. She places her fist on the table, leaning over it.

Gershom looks at her. "Why would I? It's obvious you know more than you or them are sharing with us. They're hiding things from us while also infiltrating themselves into our numbers."

"You arrogant, small-minded ass," Amara says.

I glance at Ladon, but he doesn't know their Common like I do. He and Rosalind are leaning close to each other and whispering. They're either oblivious or uninterested. Amara has had enough though.

"Small-minded!" Gershom exclaims. "I'm small-minded? I'm the only one thinking of the future! I'm not thinking with my bestial urge or sick desires! I, at least, have an eye on the long term survival of our race."

"Bestial urges?" Amara sputters.

She's so angry I think she might crawl across the table and beat Gershom. Inside I cheer her on. It would be hilarious to see her putting him in his place.

"You're an angry white man who's pissed off he can't get laid! Hell, I wouldn't fuck you if you were the last man in the damn universe!"

Gershom's face blanches, turning white, then blood flushes, and he looks purple. His mouth moves and he's spitting he's so angry. He rises from his seat, his hands balling into fists.

"You ignorant bitch," he snaps and moves around the table towards her.

Amara turns to meet his approach, showing no fear. I grab Gershom's shoulder before he can get close to her and grip him tight. He tries to ignore it and continue moving around the table but I increase the strength of my grip. Gershom whirls towards me, anger overriding his natural fear.

"Let me go you filthy animal," his voice is low and sounds like the growl of a bivo.

I smile because I know it will make him angrier but I give no outward sign I understand what he's saying.

"Let him go Shidan, I can kick his ass!" Amara says in Zmaj.

"No," I reply.

"Damn it Shidan!" She marches around the table. "Let him go."

"No, my lyutik," I say, pulling him with me as I step backwards, away from her approach. "He's not worth it."

"I will kick his smug ass!" she yells.

Taking another step backwards, my tail brushes against Ladon, forcing me to step to the side.

"Amara!" Rosalind snaps.

Amara stops mid-step, her fists still balled. Anger pulses off of her in palpable waves. She shifts her gaze from Gershom to Rosalind. Gershom squirms in my grip, trying to free himself, but I continue pretending to not understand.

"He deserves an ass kicking," Amara says, speaking Zmaj, intending to anger Gershom I'm sure.

"This is not the way to handle him," Rosalind says.

"I'm sick of his crap."

"I know," Rosalind says, simply.

She meets Amara's glare and waits, saying nothing more. The anger drains out of my treasure. She glares at Gershom a minute longer then turns and marches back to her seat without a word. Gershom is still struggling in my grip. I hold him until his weight shifts forward then let go. He stumbles forward and crashes into the table, landing in a heap on the floor. Turning over, he glares up at me so I smile.

"I agree with Gershom," Rosalind says in their human tongue, then repeats it in Zmaj for Ladon and I. "Not for the same reasons but because we need someone else who can learn the basics of engineering."

"Also part of my considerations," Gershom says, smoothing his hair on his head as he climbs to his feet.

"Then it's agreed," Rosalind says. "Shidan, Amara, and one of Gershom's choosing. Someone with mechanical aptitude Gershom."

"Oh yes," he agrees.

"How does any of this help Calista?" Ladon hisses.

His scales are darkening and his eyes are narrow slits. His wings rustle and his tail shifts side to side. He's barely controlling his anger but I doubt any of the humans know the signs. His struggle is real and very dangerous. He's glaring at Amara, so as unobtrusively as possible, I move to make sure I'm between them.

"I don't know," Amara says, meeting his gaze.

Silence sits heavy in the room. Ladon glares, his wings rustle and his tail sweeps wider. Ladon is bigger than I am, a warrior which I never had the chance to become, but it doesn't matter. I'm smaller and faster. I'll use it to my advantage. He will not harm her.

"Then why do it? You said we need equipment, there must be more in this city. Something that is undamaged." His voice is soft, his eyes narrow, and his hands ball into fists.

"Because even if we find equipment that's working, I don't know if we can power it," Amara replies. "We have the dome working and intermittent lights. Since the dome came up, everything else is out. The dome is taking all the power the city can generate."

"Do you think I am unaware of this?" Ladon hisses.

"No," Amara says. "I think you are focused on Calista, which you should be."

"What else should I *focus* on?"

"Nothing, that's the point. Let me handle this," Amara says, her voice earnest.

"Why won't you people speak in Common!" Gershom interrupts.

Ladon moves fast, faster than I would have expected. His arm shoots out and he grabs Gershom by the front of his shirt, jerking him to his feet and raising him off the ground to eye level. He hisses in Gershom's face. Gershom trembles in Ladon's grip, his entire body spasming.

"Ladon!" Rosalind barks.

"Ladon, this isn't the way," Amara adds.

I can't believe she's defending Gershom, but that is my Amara. Her heart is too big for her small body.

"Speak again tiny human," Ladon hisses.

Gershom's eyes widen further still. He splutters in response, no words coming from his lips.

Amara bursts into motion. I reach for her but she slips past my grip. In an instant she's next to Ladon.

"Amara!" I yell.

Ignoring me, she places a hand on Ladon's arm. I leap onto the table to reach her faster but time slows to a crawl. She touches him and he turns towards her as my foot moves through the thick air. Fear pounds through my body, flooding my mind with hyper-awareness.

"Ladon, don't do this," Amara says. "Please."

Ladon shudders from his head to the tip of his tail. He drops Gershom who stumbles, landing on his backside. Ladon stares at Amara then the tension drops away.

"Fine," he says. "Do what you must, but hurry."

He storms out of the room, slamming the door open so hard it cracks against the wall. Everyone stands in stunned silence. Amara watches him leave but I have eyes only for her. She stood up to Ladon, two or three times her size, with no fear. His anger meant nothing to her. She saw through his

43

anger to the pain beneath it and with her beautiful heart, she defused him. A halo of light surrounds her as she turns to face those of us still in the room.

Feeling awkward I climb off of the table and go to stand next to her. Gershom climbs back to his feet huffing and puffing. Rosalind watches everything, impassive as ever.

"See!" Gershom says. "This is what I've been trying to tell you people. They're animals! Dirty, filthy, dangerous animals!"

"Gershom," Rosalind warns.

"What?"

"Shut up," she says. Amara snorts. "Pick your person. I want this project done, we don't have time to waste."

"Fine," Gershom says, straightening his clothes then marching out.

"I hope you're right about this," Rosalind says to Amara.

"Me too," she says, looking over her shoulder to where Ladon left the broken door. "She's my friend."

Rosalind nods then leaves. At last the two of us are alone. I hope, maybe, she might express gratitude for my handling of Gershom. Perhaps she might at last let me past the barriers she has erected. My imagination runs wild with the idea she might come into my arms and how soft she will feel. I'll wrap myself around her and enfold her in my wings, protecting her from all the world. Treasuring her perfection.

She turns on one heel, looking up at me, a frown on her beautiful, perfect face.

"Don't do that," she says, crossing her arms over her chest.

"What?" I ask.

"Try to protect me," she says. "Don't. I don't need it."

"I don't understand," I say in confusion. This is not what I expected.

"I know," she says, her lips pursing as her brow furrows in deep thought. She shakes her head. "Just don't," she says. "I'm not your treasure. I'm not the one, okay? Just... pick someone else. Someone better."

"There is no one— "

"No!" she raises her voice, shaking her head as she cuts me off. "Don't say it. I'm not the one, got it? There are lots of other girls, any of them would be better for you than me."

"But— "

"No, no buts," she says, stamping her foot on the ground. "Damn it, no!"

Moisture wells in the corners of her eyes, her face is flushing red. I don't understand. Why is she upset? What have I done? Biting down hard to keep myself from saying more, I nod.

"Good," she says, shaking her head. "Now let's go see who the douche bag picked to come with us."

"What's a douche bag?" I ask, confused by the words.

Amara looks at me over her shoulder in disbelief then shakes her head. "Forget it, I will not explain that one to you," she says, then heads out the door.

Confusion whirls in my mind like a storm of sand. I'm frustrated. Every time I think I've impressed her it goes wrong, but it doesn't matter. A treasure is worth fighting for and I will, nothing will stop me.

5

AMARA

The gall!

Storming down the street, anger pulses in every beat of my heart. The hair on my arms stands on end as I grind my teeth in frustration. I'm pissed at Gershom but almost as much at Shidan. If he hadn't stopped me, I'd have kicked Gershom's lily-white ass all over this planet. I don't need anyone stepping in to fight my battles for me.

Sweat drips into my eyes and I wipe at it furiously. It's too hot to be mad. Stopping, I lift the bottom of my shirt and wipe sweat away from my eyes. Two deep breaths, in and out. Fine, he was trying to help. I get that but I don't want his help. I won't let him in. I won't. I don't need him. I don't need anyone, I'm better off alone.

Resuming my walk, my tool bag bangs against my side with every step. I've brought more than I will ever need, but it's better to be prepared than to be outside wishing I had something. Still, all these tools will be useless unless I find something to use them on.

Slowly I form a plan. We'll start with the box. If that proves fruitless then maybe it will at least give me a clue to something else. More sweat runs down my face and I'm not even outside the dome yet. I really hate this planet. I've decided it's not Tatooine or Vulcan. It's just hell. Maybe that's it, I died in the wreck of the ship and this is my shitty afterlife.

I sure as hell don't feel like Luke Skywalker or Captain Kirk. End of the day it sucks here. It's hot all the damn time, even after taking epis, the plant that's supposed to make it so we can survive here. I'm hot, sweaty, and sticky, always. Maybe if I could figure out how to get power flowing to this wreck of a city, we could have air conditioning. I dream of a temperature lower than one hundred degrees. That would be heaven.

Or showers! What I would give for a nice, warm shower. Hot, cleansing water beating down on my skin, eases tension from muscles. Scrubbing myself clean. Damn I miss showers.

Turning a corner, the edge of the city and the shimmer of the dome is just a few blocks ahead. The protective shield looks amber in the reflected light of double suns. The dome keeps wandering monsters at bay and here on Tajss that's a very necessary thing. Monsters are real. It also reduces radiation from the suns and thereby the heat. Before we got it working the temperature was even hotter.

There's only one working airlock through the dome, so far as we know. This one is man sized, well Zmaj sized. There are others around the dome, some of which would be big enough for vehicles, but none of those are operational. Standing next to the airlock is a guy I don't know. He's middle-aged, broad shouldered, and has a craggy face that looks like he took a beating and the swelling is just going down. He's dressed stupid, too, in a tight red shirt that looks like it's made of cotton. Most of us have learned to dress in loose layers which helps keep us cool. I don't know if this guy is too dumb to have figured that trick out or just to masochistic to give into the demands of his environment. Either way it's dumb.

"Hi," he says as I walk up.

"Hey," I say, looking around for Shidan.

"I'm Mark," he says, extending his hand out, waiting.

"Fine," I say, still looking around.

I stop looking around and stare at his hand, then at him. He has a fixed smile and his small, beady eyes stare with a vapid look. I arch an eyebrow then take his hand. It's sweaty and gross so I let go as fast as I can. One tenet of Gershom's followers is that they refuse to take epis.

See? Stupid. Epis is life on this planet. Literally. It's a plant harvested in caverns made from the passage of creatures that look like a cross between a giant earth worm and a monster with too many teeth. Think Tremors. Good old "Six Degrees of Kevin Bacon".

The Zmaj call the worms zemlja, or earth dragons. I've only heard stories about them and would prefer not to have a run in with one. Their excrement enriches the soil and in that soil only, the epis grows. It has unique properties that does a lot of science talk stuff. Jolie and Calista were botanists so they like to go on and on about what it does, but all I know is the basics. It changes you on a genetic level adjusting your body so you can handle the heat of Tajss. It also, at least in theory, extends your life, or seems to for the Zmaj. No one knows yet the long term effects on humans. The downside is, once you've taken it you can never leave Tajss. If you don't take epis regularly you go into withdrawals which will kill you. I try not to think about that part too much. Survive today and figure tomorrow out when it gets here.

Mark has a backpack and several canteens. He'll need even more than I will since he hasn't taken epis. Because he's an idiot and probably a bigot and a xenophobe but hey, who am I to judge? Sweat pours down his face like a waterfall and we haven't even gone outside the dome yet. Almost, I feel sorry for him. If it wasn't his choice, I would. It's not like he doesn't know the situation. He made his choices.

"You're Amara?" he asks.

"Yes," I say, resuming looking for Shidan who I expected to be here already.

He's always here. This is the first time I can remember since he showed up that I can turn around and he isn't right in my damn way. Now I want him and he's not here. Typical.

"Pleasure to meet you," Mark says. "What are we waiting for?"

"Shidan."

"Oh," he says, sounding disappointed.

I glance at him over my shoulder. He's staring at the ground and pursing his lips. "What?"

"He's... he's one of them isn't he?"

"Yeah, what of it?" I growl.

"Nothing," he says without looking up.

"Yeah, right, what?"

"Are you and him...," he trails off, glancing up to my face.

"Are you kidding me?"

"Hey, I was just, you know, asking."

"Sure, you were just, you know, asking. Right. What if I am? What if I'm banging the holy hell out of that big alien dragon man? Taking his sweet alien cock and riding it all damn night long. What of it?"

"Nothing, I mean, it's... well it's just— " he splutters, wide-eyed, shaking his head furiously as he tries to find words.

"Yeah, it's just," I say.

Suddenly, he backs away two stumbling steps. I know, without turning around, why. Shidan. God damn if he doesn't have the worst timing in the entire fucking world!

Did he hear me? My cheeks burn hot and every muscle tenses in embarrassment but then I remember Shidan doesn't speak Common. Relief floods through me so hard and fast a shudder runs down my spine. Thank baby Jesus he didn't hear me talking about riding his cock. I don't think I'd ever be able to look him in the eye again.

"Where the hell have you been?" I ask, whirling on Shidan, harsher than I intended because of my embarrassment.

"I was getting supplies, my lyutik."

"Don't call me that!"

"As you wish."

He smiles so I shake my head. "Let's go," I say, in both Common and Zmaj. What a pain in the ass it is to have to speak in two languages. "Mark, right?" I ask the red shirt.

"Yes," he says, brightening. Apparently he's excited that I remembered his name.

"Do you speak Zmaj?" I ask. His crestfallen face is all the answer I need. "Of course not, fuck my life."

Before he can say anything further, I go to the airlock and punch in the code to let us out of the dome. The door opens with a swoosh and I usher the two men through before entering. As I do, the door closes, air hissing as the pressure equalizes to the outside. The temperature rises as the process takes place, rising to what it is outside.

"Damn it's hot," Mark says, wiping his arm across his forehead.

"No shit?" I comment, and he looks at me like he's hurt.

Arching an eyebrow I look up and down his outfit. He looks down then shrugs. He keeps glancing at Shidan sidelong and I know I'm in for a very long day. The outer lock door opens and we exit. The box I'm wanting to investigate is relatively close so we trudge our way towards it.

Jolie excavated part of it before but time has passed. I

imagine that the surface of Tajss would look different from space every other day. The sands are constantly shifting in the hot breeze. What was a two feet deep hole the last time I was here is now barely an indentation in the sand. Directing the two men to help, we clear sand away from the box until I can see all around it. Mark stops for frequent water breaks, which is good I guess, without epis and in that outfit I'll be lucky if he doesn't get heat stroke before we get this part of the job finished.

Pulling my tool bag closer to the edge of the hole we've dug out, I crouch down beside the box. There are bolts on each corner around the top. I select a wrench and hook it onto a bolt then lean into it. It doesn't move. Shidan's shadow covers me, giving me some welcome relief from the direct heat of the suns.

"Allow me," Shidan says, leaning in.

Part of me wants to tell him no, but that'd be stupid. He's big, and he's strong, why wouldn't I use that to our advantage? Instead, I nod and climb out of the hole, giving him room to get down next to the box.

Shidan takes the wrench in both hands and strains. His muscles bulge and flex as he leans, applying his not inconsiderable strength. Mark stands to one side watching. He's been all but useless, as I expected, but it still irritates me. He's so busy wiping sweat away from his eyes with a rag he doesn't seem to have time to pay attention or be helpful.

There's a loud screech then Shidan 'oofs' and falls forward, his wings spreading out to break his fall. Mark jumps back, his eyes going wide as one of Shidan's wings brushes across his midsection. Shidan lands over the box, catching himself before he plants his face in the sand. I laugh before I can stop it. Shidan looks over his shoulder at me as his wings fold against his back. He smiles as he climbs to his feet.

"Got it," he grins.

"So you did," I agree, laughing.

Shidan is always so good-natured. A lot of guys would have gotten pissed being laughed at but not Shidan. He's different. My core tightens and a deeply suppressed emptiness aches inside me looking at his smiling face. No. I can't and I won't. I won't let anyone else suffer for me, but maybe I can help Shidan find someone who would be good for him.

Shidan rolls his shoulders then moves to the next bolt. Putting the wrench on it carefully, he pulls it towards him this time which works much better. This one gives way under his ministration and then he's on to the next. He finishes loosening the bolts with no further misadventure.

"Mark, can you help him lift that lid?" I ask, pointing down into the hold.

Mark looks at me, slack-jawed and wide-eyed. "Down there?" he asks, pointing into the hole.

"You see a lid somewhere else?" I don't get his problem.

"No," he says, actually looking around like there might be one suddenly appearing out of the sand or something.

Slapping a hand to my forehead I sigh in utter frustration. "What?"

"He's there," Mark says, his face getting even redder than his sunburn.

"Yes, yes he is, very observant. If you hadn't noticed, 'he' as you call him, just got the stuck bolts loose by himself. 'He' also cleared most of the sand away and in general 'he' has done more than his share. You have moistened the sand with your sweat."

"I helped," Mark says, hands flying up and fluttering in the air in what I assume is meant to be a defensive gesture.

Biting my tongue I stop. I will not engage, just get the damn help I need.

"Yes, thank you," I say, doing my damn best to keep frustration out of my voice. "Now can you please help, one more time, and take a corner of that lid?"

Mark swallows hard, but he nods. "Okay."

He climbs down into the hole. It's obvious he's trying to stay as far away from Shidan as possible, but considering it's a four foot wide hole it's futile. I translate to Shidan what I want then both of them grab the lid. They lift and slide it to one side and the three of us stare into the box.

At nothing.

"Shit," Mark says.

"Yeah," I agree.

Sand and gray dust cover the bottom of the box. Whatever was in there has rotted away. There's a hole in either side that leads out, like some kind of conduits going somewhere. One leads out across the desert and one back under the dome. The question is, what the hell was in here and what was its purpose? I fall back onto my haunches and stare.

"This does not look right," Shidan says.

"You think?" I ask.

"I do," he smiles. "There should be wires and a machine in here."

"Do you know anything about this stuff?"

Shidan shrugs. "No," he admits. "But I've helped enough in your work to know what kind of things should be there."

"Great, thanks," I roll my eyes.

"What did he say?" Mark asks.

"He said you look tasty, and he's thinking you might make a nice snack," I bite off the words, not expecting Mark to take them seriously.

He does though. His eyes widen as his head snaps around towards Shidan and he backpedals. The sand slides under his feet causing him to trip and fall over. He's still scrambling backwards in a crab-crawl while Shidan stares, tilting his head to one side.

"Is he okay?" Shidan asks. "Has the heat affected his mind?"

"He's fine," I say, laughing so hard tears form in my eyes. "He thinks you want to eat him."

"Why would he think this?"

"Because I told him that's what you said," I say, wiping tears of laughter from my eyes.

"Oh," he looks at Mark and a grin spreads across his face. He snaps his wings wide and raises his arms over his head showing sharp nails. Taking a step forward he hisses. Mark crab-crawls backwards even faster, a 'huh-huh-huh' sound coming out of him and I can see he's about to hyperventilate.

"Please, I'm not tasty, please, no!" Mark cries, crawling backwards as fast as he can.

"Oh damn it Mark, stand up, we're screwing with you!" I yell, giving in at last.

Still crawling backwards, Mark looks over at me as I laugh. Realizing that Shidan isn't coming any closer, he drops to the ground, his chest heaving. Slowly Mark climbs to his feet, dusts himself off, but keeps his distance from Shidan.

"You're sure?" he asks, looking at me but holding his head to keep Shidan in his field of vision.

"Would I lie to you?" I grin.

He glares at me then at Shidan. "That shit isn't funny."

"Right," I agree, trying to compose my face. "I'm sorry," I say but a snicker slips out.

Mark glares resentfully, but it's the least he deserves. Racist ass. Besides, I haven't had that good of a laugh in a long time. Shidan chuckles as I come to stand next to him.

"He's a funny man," Shidan observes.

"He's an asshole," I say.

Having had my fun, I climb up a nearby dune of red sand. The view is stunning. Red sand striated with varying shades of red cut by lines of white for as far as the eye can see. The hot, dry breeze shifts the sand making new patterns all the way to the horizon. The double suns cause the sand to sparkle like tiny shards of glass strewn across the land. It's beautiful, in a barren, lifeless kind of way. And it looks more like Vulcan. Tatooine was yellow, this red shit is Vulcan, all the way. I have to remember to point that out the girls when I get home.

"What do you think lyutik?" Shidan asks, climbing the dune to stand next to me.

"That those tubes go somewhere, we have to figure out where and to what."

"Very insightful."

I glance over to see if he's being a smart ass, but he seems sincere.

"What are we doing?" Mark asks, joining us and carefully keeping me between him and Shidan.

"Do you have any idea how much easier life would be if you would just learn the fucking language?" I snap.

"Why should I have to?" he snarks back.

"Because it's their damn planet! Have you thought about that? Here, we're the aliens, not them. We crashed into them, not the other way around."

"Whatever," he says, shaking his head and turning away.

"Idiot," I sigh.

Maybe he can't help it. It's obvious he's scared. I could be less of a bitch to him but damn it he rubs me the wrong way. Whirling on my heel, I bump into Shidan, who once again, is right in my space.

"Damn it, Shidan," I growl.

"Apologies, my lyutik," he says, nodding his head.

"Let's go," I say twice so they both understand.

We start across the desert in more or less a straight line, trying to follow the direction the tubes went.

We don't make it far before the heat settles in. It's hot. So damn hot. My throat is dry and scratchy, my skin burns despite my protective layers. Taking the epis helps, a lot, but it doesn't solve the problem. Human bodies don't function well in temperatures like this, even with the changes caused by the epis. It's been a while since I took my last dosage too. It's dangerous to harvest so supplies are very limited. There's also no way to preserve it for long. Maybe it's a good thing that Gershom and his followers like Mark here refuse to take it. More for those of us who are facing the reality that this is our new home.

There's no hope of rescue. This is it. Welcome home, now make the best of it. Or don't. Your choice.

The suns beats down mercilessly as we march. Despite his size, Shidan has an easier time moving across the sand than Mark or I, which just isn't fair. He outweighs both of us together but his body is made for this. He spreads his wings, uses his tail as a guide and runs across the sand like Legolas across snow while Mark and I have to fight for every forward step. It's exhausting.

Mark is having an even rougher time of it. His face is as red as his bright shirt, his skin is peeling and his eyes are sunken. All signs of extreme dehydration. I might feel sorry for him if he wasn't so unbelievably stupid in the first place.

"Wait," Mark pants, hands on his knees.

He takes out another water bottle and downs it. Sweat is pouring out of him as fast as he can drink. He takes salt and potassium pills but it won't be enough. It might keep him functioning but barely. He'll have a heat stroke before long. Stupid idiot.

Looking back, we're out of sight of the city. Dunes of sand block off any sight of the dome.

"You shouldn't be out here," I observe.

"No choice," he says, then downs more water.

"Why not?"

Shidan moves next to me and the flapping of his wings makes a nice breeze. Mark looks over my shoulder at Shidan then back at me.

"We need to be sure," he says.

"Sure of what?"

"That we're not being left out," he says, leaning his head back and pouring more water across his face.

"Out of what? Shit, say what you mean man. It's like pulling teeth to figure out what you're saying!"

Mark rubs his face then shakes his head, flinging droplets of water across me. It's disgusting so I step back and bump into Shidan. The sand sinks under my feet at the same time and I stumble, losing my balance. Shidan's strong hands close on my arms and hold me upright. I pull out of his grip, giving him a quick glare over my shoulder. He smiles, like he always does. I roll my eyes.

"Look, it's obvious that there are two camps of survivors. Those who embrace the aliens and want to interbreed with them and those of us who remember our greater mission. Our job is to find and populate a planet. For humans. We don't want to be left out of the planning. We want to fulfill our obligation to our ancestors."

"But the mission is dead," I say. "We crashed, we're here, not where we're supposed to be. Our target was an uninhabited planet terraformed and ready for our arrival. That's not happening. This is it. We'll never see that planet. I like to call this, welcome to reality."

"You don't know that," he says petulantly. "And it doesn't change our obligation. We are the hope of the human race. It's our duty to make sure that humans survive."

"As opposed to?"

He looks at Shidan. "We want to make sure we survive. I want a family, kids, and a life that's better than this for them," he says.

I want to be angry at him. I want to hate him or tell Shidan to beat him up or something. I want to be but I'm not and I don't. He's scared, that's more than obvious. He wants a family and kids, can I blame him for that even if he is a small-minded, racist bigot? And his fear is palpable because all of that is slipping away and he can't do anything about it.

"Just-" I raise and lower my hands trying to find words for my feelings. Nothing comes so I shake my head, dropping my hands to my side. "Screw it, let's get going."

Mark shrugs and we resume our march. I stop after a while and dig down into the sand while directing Mark and Shidan to do the same twenty feet to either side. We work our way towards each other until we find the tube and realign ourselves along its apparent path.

I'm running out of water. This is the stupidest idea ever. I'm marching towards something that may not even exist. Or more likely it's already destroyed or rotted away. Even if I find it, I probably won't have any idea what to do with it. Dumb, but I keep on marching. I'm running out of ideas and right now this is the best I can do. Calista needs me and the entire damn city is counting on me to fix the stupid power.

Mark weaves side to side as he walks, wandering further off to one side but he keeps moving. I feel bad for him. I remember what it was like before I took epis. The constant headache, the desire to sleep, every muscle in my body hurting. Dehydration is a slow, secret killer you don't even realize it's destroying you. I may not be able to leave Tajss because I have to take epis regularly but at least I'm not suffering, not like I know Mark is.

"Mark!" I yell as he stumbles along, heading for some bright orange flowers.

He spins around and looks my way then waves, weaving back and forth.

"These are pretty," he says, pointing at the colorful blooms.

He moves closer to the flowers and then a cloudy mist bursts from the plant, engulfing Mark. His face changes, going from miserable and beet red to a broad smile with wide eyes. He points up into the sky and cries out excitedly. There are no words but it sounds joyous.

"They've come!" he says, jumping up and down, waving his arms wildly in the air.

I run. I don't know what's going on but there's nothing on this hell hole that isn't out to kill you. The loose sand pulls my feet down with each step.

"MARK!" I yell.

Slow, too slow.

"Amara, no!" Shidan yells, but I ignore him.

Mark turns and looks at me, still grinning like an idiot. "Amara, it's home, we made it! They came for us! We're being rescued."

I'm close enough now to see he's in the middle of a small field of the bright orange flowers. Thick, brown vines run between them lying across the sand. The flowers tremble and my gut sinks. Something bad is about to happen, I know it. I could really use my nerdtastic botanist friends right about now.

"Mark, damn it, get out of there!"

"It's okay," he says. "I'm just going to... lie down here a minute. They'll carry me to the ships."

Damn it. I shouldn't have let him get so far away. It was my bright idea to spread us out so we could have a better chance of catching sight of any machinery. I'm sinking halfway up my calf with each forward step. Shidan's wings flap behind me as he comes closer but I'm not waiting for him, I've got to get to Mark. He's an idiot, but he doesn't deserve to die.

Mark's smile is fixed on his face and his eyes are on the sky. The vines, as thick as my forearm, crawl up his legs, wrapping around him.

"MARK!" I scream so loud it feels like my throat tears.

He doesn't look my way or react to the sound of my voice. He's lost in a world of his own. I don't know what's happening but I know it's bad. The vines climb up his legs, wrapping around him, now reaching his waist. The flowers tremble, all of them, the entire field as if they're all part of one organism.

Suddenly Mark screams. Its blood-curdling, filled with pain and agony as the vines wrap around his chest. He doesn't struggle, just screams with that god-awful vacant smile on his face. I stumble through the flowers to him, grabbing one vine that's wrapped around his chest. I pull with everything I've got, fighting with it. There's a sick tearing sound as I peel it back and blood drips from it.

Son of a bitch it's drinking him!

I look over my shoulder to yell for Shidan. He's a short distance away coming closer. He's yelling too but the air fills with a burning mist that goes up my nose. It races right into my brain and then I'm tired. So, so tired. I turn a slow circle as the desert wavers then fades away.

"Stancher! Apollo!" Lieutenant Daniels barks.

"Yes sir!" we say in unison. I stiffen my attention even further if that's possible.

Ben has been my Lead and I his Wingman since I made it into flight deck. Lieutenant Daniels stands in front of the line of pilots with a clipboard in hand. The results of a new training program. Only a handful of us will make the cut and be Top Flight. The rest will go back to standard patrols and maintenance. He's already called out four pairs. There's only one slot left.

"You've made it," he says. Pride swells as the men to either side of me groan. "Rest of you pasty-ass, dog-face, stick-jockeys pay attention. Stancher can teach all of you something. She didn't just beat you, she blew you all out of the water."

He walks over to stand in front of us and then places the Top Flight Wings on my uniform.

"Now take a nap Stancher," he orders. "You two are on deck next so get yourself ready. You've set a high bar. Don't you let me down!"

"Sir, yes, sir!" I salute.

"Dismissed!" he barks.

The men and I fall out.

"We did it," Ben turns grinning from ear to ear.

"Yeah," I say, shaking my head. "Part of me can't believe we made the cut."

"Never a doubt in my mind," Ben says. "You're the best wing-woman a man can have."

He grips my shoulder. It's the closest we ever come to intimacy. Ben and I's relationship isn't like that. Not that he's not good looking enough, but I don't want to affect our flying. Nothing is more important than that. Not to mention the regulations strictly forbid it.

I do my best to ignore the mutterings of those who didn't make the cut as they walk away. They glower and grouse but that's the end of it. I'm used to it. I know what they think but they can kiss my ass. I can out fly all of them. Then Draker walks over. Draker and I have become enemies over the past year. It went downhill fast as soon as Ben Apollo dumped him as his wingman in favor of me. Jackson, his new wingman, swaggers next to Draker and a few other pilots hang close to see what will happen next. Everyone knows he hates me and of our rivalry. I've even heard of betting pools on which one of us will come out on top. Unfortunately these two made the cut to Top Flight as well.

"So, Stancher," Draker says, stopping in front of me.

Jackson glares at me over his shoulder.

"Leave her alone Draker," Ben says.

"Stay out of it pretty boy," Draker snaps. "Tell me, Stancher, what favors did you give the old man to make the cut?"

Draker's voice is soft and vile. The men watching him snicker, muttering. They close the circle around Ben and I as if on a silent cue. Someone shoulders into me, knocking me off balance. Catching myself, I stand up straight again and meet Draker's gaze.

"Back off Draker," I say.

"Back off?" he asks. "Back off of what. No woman can do what you did, hell most men can't do what you claim. The G's of that maneuver would black out anyone. I know you've rigged the machines somehow. That's why you're always hanging with Tomas and the other mech grubs isn't it? Cozy up to them and then they rig the readouts for you. Maybe you do the same 'favors' for them?"

Out of nowhere Ben swings at Draker. Draker ducks then Jackson is there and chaos erupts. Something hits me hard in the chest and I'm knocked backwards. Draker and Ben are pulled apart by several of the onlookers.

"I'll take you on any time Draker!" I scream.

"Sure Stancher, I want to be the one who shows up the Lieutenant's pet," he barks. "Besides, aren't you tired? You look tired. You can't keep your eyes open."

I am tired. So damn tired but never too tired to put this punk piece of shit in his place. "I can out fly you with one hand tied behind my seat."

He snorts jerking free of the guys holding him.

"Whatever Stancher," he says. "I know you cheated. I'll figure out how sooner or later."

Something behind him catches my eye. It's out of place here on the flight deck. A big man with wings. No wait, he has scales, and he's staring at me. There's something intriguing about him, something familiar. Weird. I must be dreaming.

"I don't cheat Draker," I bark.

"No one," Draker says, whirling around on me, "and I mean no one, can do what you say you did. I'm on to your game and I'm not the only one."

Everyone is glaring at me. Not one of them sticks up for me. Every single one of them looks at me with resentment in their eyes. Even Ben looks doubtful. Shame and anger burn hot inside then my cheeks flush. Anger floods behind the embarrassment. They can't know Draker's getting to me. I didn't cheat, damn it. Fighting an urge to scream, because I know that will make me look weak, I clench my fists. Unable to go on the defensive I go offensive.

"Anytime you think you're man enough you grub," I bark at Draker. "I'll take on you or anyone you care to put forward. I earned my damn wings."

The dragon-man smiles and nods, he's at the far side of the flight deck and coming closer, walking through the crew but none of them seem to notice him. Why is that? What the hell is he doing here? Do we allow aliens on the ship? Isn't that against regs?

"You wouldn't dare," Draker laughs.

"Try me!" I yell. "You scared? Afraid I'll show you up? Put your money where your mouth is."

He blanches and I know I'm on the right track. Even the guys with him look at him now, putting the pressure on him to meet my challenge.

"Fine!" he barks, but his voice quavers.

It's not much but I don't miss it. He's scared because he knows he doesn't have the goods to out fly me.

The dragon-man is yelling something. What is he saying? Oh, that's my name. How does the dragon-man know my name? The lights flicker and everything goes dark before lighting up. Suppressing a yawn, I shake my head to clear it.

I'm tired. So, so tired...

6

SHIDAN

*T*he vines of the ioza wrap her legs and reach her middle before I can close the distance between us. It was stupid to spread out so far. I should have known better. What was I was thinking? Never should have allowed her to be so far from me outside the dome. Running across the sand as fast as I can, she's deep in the throes of the ioza's hallucinogen.

She's saying something I can't make out. Mark has fallen to the ground and Amara is being pulled down when I reach her. If the vines get around her, I don't know if I'll be able to save her. Drawing my lochaber, a long staff with a metal sword end, I run, whirling it to ready. Once I'm close enough, I leap into the air, spread my wings wide, and glide past the outer roots of the ioza to land close to Amara.

Swinging my lochaber with one hand, I grab her with my free arm. The blade swings below her body, hitting into the thick vines of the ioza. The blade contacts and cuts part way in then sends a numbing vibration up my arm. My grip on the lochaber spasms but I can't let go, through will alone I maintain my grip. The ioza reacts to the attack, filling the air with its spores. Surrounded by them, I close my protective lenses over my eyes and hold my breath.

One handed, I work the lochaber free of the vines and swing it again but the ioza attacks. Vines entwine my feet, forcing me to keep stepping to avoid being trapped while I work to free her. It throws off my center and keeps me from bringing my full strength to bear. I strike once more but again fail to cut through. A vine wraps around my left foot and pulls, trying to trip me to the ground.

Desperation swells. Swinging again, I cut through some of the vines but more race to take their place. The flowers vibrate as the plant realizes I'm a threat. Amara is quiet and out. The situation worsens with each passing moment. I have to get her away before it's too late.

An idea comes full fledged, crazy, but it's the only chance I have. Letting her go I grab my lochaber with both hands, bend in half at my waist, then swing with everything I have at the vines holding her. Bringing my full strength to bear, the lochaber slices through. Fresh vines race up to replace them but I exhale a ball of fire as the lochaber severs them. The vines pull back from my flames.

I grab Amara before she drops to the ground, spread my wings, and run. Vines wrap my foot, stopping me in place with a jerk. Amara slips in my arms and I scrabble to hold on to her before she falls. The vines resume their attack. I can't breathe fire again, I have no air left. I'm light-headed from needing to breathe but I can't. If I inhale the spores, I'll fall into hallucinations as well.

Shifting her to my other arm, I pull her up so she's lying over my shoulder. Taking my lochaber in my other hand, I lean forward, pulling against the restraining vine then swing backward and free my foot. A careful dance from foot to foot and I'm free of most of them. Moving Amara back into my arms to free my wings I spread them and run until I'm sure I'm clear of the plant's reach.

The ioza has settled, hiding most of its vines under the sand as if nothing happened. The only ones in sight have wrapped Mark from head to toe. There's nothing I can do to save him. If I go back in there, we'll both be dead and I'm sure he's already gone. The ioza survives off the blood of creatures unfortunate enough to fall into its reach.

Kneeling next to Amara, I look her over for anything that needs immediate treatment. She's feverish, sweaty, and shivering despite the heat. Damn. I don't know how her body will handle the spores. A strong Zmaj can survive them but would need rest and nutrition. A human? There is no choice but for me to get her back to the city as fast as possible. Someone there will help her.

Gathering her into my arms I turn and run. She's light and I can't deny it's a pleasure to feel her close. How long I have dreamed of this but never under such circumstances. The moment I saw her outside the dome so many cycles ago I knew. The longing, driving, deep down desire awakened as soon as I laid eyes on her. I had to have her. She was the one.

Even now her hair tickles along my side as I run. It bounces almost as if it has a life of its own. I run as fast as I can and it dances in the breeze. She's soft. So, so soft. I've only touched her in momentary passing, enough to know her skin is silky but holding her! There is a smoothness to her legs, her hips, her side. All seem delicate and gentle. Yet I know she is as tough as the scales of any Zmaj.

She must be all right, has to be. I will save her.

She is my treasure whether she accepts this yet or not. I am worthy and I will prove it to her. My devotion will not waver. Now though, focus. Push away thoughts of the future, of the past, focus in the now. One foot in front of another.

My wings mustn't stop working. The sand wants to pull me in, slow me down, but I will not weaken.

We've come far from Drakonov, the city. Over half a day's journey. I left my supplies where I dropped them when I ran to save her so I have no water. Exhaustion threatens my muscles but I will not give in. I will not fail her. She is my lyutik. I will see her through this trial. Bowing my head I run, leaning in. I bound, using my wings to carry me forward and my tail to keep myself from losing balance. My muscles tremble, aching with exertion, but my will keeps my flesh from giving in.

The suns set, casting long shadows across the dunes. Amara convulses in my arms. I have to slow down to make sure I don't drop her as her body struggles against whatever she is dreaming. She moans and cries out then stiffens and quiets. Hold on my lyutik. We are not far.

Every step is hard. My legs are heavy, my wings hurt, every beat is a screaming, shooting sensation that burns through my chest. My arms quiver with exhaustion but I don't let myself slow. I will save her. Somehow. I'm climbing a dune that seems to go forever. Her breathing has become even and steady. That's good, I hope. I have to let the muscles of my wings rest so I fold them in. Carrying her along with my weight causes me to sink into the sand. Every step is struggle but I push through it. Reaching the top, the glimmer of the city dome is in the distance.

Hope wars with the sinking in my stomach. It's far, much farther than I hoped. Bowing my head I dig deep into my resolve. I heft Amara up to a better position and take a moment to look at her. Her dry, cracked lips mutter. She's bright red and feverish. Feeling bold I kiss her forehead.

"Hang in lyutik, we are almost home," I whisper.

I run. Digging deep, I find reserves of strength I didn't know were in me. Coming down the dune I pick up speed. I spread my wings with a pop and use my forward momentum to leap and glide, giving my other muscles much needed respite. I'm running as soon as my feet hit the ground. One step after another. I climb another dune and repeat the pattern coming down the far side. As I land after a long glide, the ground beneath me rumbles.

Damn! I drop to a crouch, pulling Amara close to my chest then go still. The sand shifts down the dune in front of me in a slide. There's a tremble in the earth, its subtle, the zemlja must be deep but that won't stop it from detecting any motion. The senses of a zemlja are legendary. Bowing my head, I offer my hopes to the stars. If I must fight a zemlja for her, alone, I will but I'm not a fool. Having a full grown zemlja as an opponent while trying to make sure she remains safe will kill us both.

The sand stops shifting. Gone or not I wait. A few moments of patience could mean the difference between life and death. The sand runs again, it's moving, then the sand is running faster. I tense but hold my position. If I move it will come for us.

In the distance there's an explosion as the zemlja bursts from the ground. The heavy dusk and the dunes block my vision of it coming through but I hear a scream as it claims its prey then the ground rocks as it buries its way back underground. The running sand slows then stops. I wait a few minutes to be sure then take a tentative step forward. Nothing happens so I take two more steps then stop. Silence. A few more steps, stop, then a few more until I'm satisfied the zemlja has moved on. Only then do I resume my dead run for the city.

"We're almost home Amara," I say. "Soon my lyutik."

She doesn't react, but I didn't expect her to. The grip of the ioza is strong. She will be deep in hallucinations of a better world. Something that makes her happy and content so that the plant can drain her without struggle. I wonder if I am in her dream? Ridiculous but it's a nice thought. She will see, in time, that we belong together.

I'm on the verge of collapse when I climb a hill and come up short. The city is right here. Renewed vigor fills me and I run along the dome, looking for the airlock that will allow us access. When I find it people show up on the other side.

"What is happening?" some human I don't know yells, but he's speaking their tongue not mine so I ignore him.

The door opens with a swoosh and I step in. It closes behind me then I have to wait as the air equalizes inside and out before it will let us through. By the time I emerge a crowd has gathered. Do these humans have nothing better to do than gather in mindless mobs?

"Clear the way!" I hiss, pushing through them.

I need Jolie or Calista. They're among the only ones I trust to care for Amara. Or Rosalind. Rosalind will know what to do, somehow. I must get to them. The crowd pushes in around me, forced forward by those behind trying to see. They all talk, making a cacophony of voices and shifting bodies.

Anger flashes through me white hot. Instinct roars and the urge to kill them for being in my way pulses with each beating of my hearts.

"MOVE!" I scream, and most of them fall back, creating an opening I push through without hesitation.

As I rush forward, I see a flash of white. Ahead of me Rosalind rushes up with Sverre at her side. The crowd is pushing up from behind and jostling against me.

"She needs help!" I scream at Rosalind.

"What's happened?" she asks.

"Ioza plant," I say to Sverre.

"Oh no," Sverre says, his scales edge green with concern.

"We have to help her, I don't know how this will affect her," I say and even I hear the note of begging in my voice.

"Where's Mark?" Gershom asks, pushing through the crowd. He looks at Amara then me.

I ignore him because I'm not supposed to know their language. Besides, I don't like him and right now he's just another barrier in my way of getting help for Amara. Sverre moves closer but the crowd of humans is pushing in close, jostling me. Someone hits into me from behind hard enough I stumble forward. My grip on Amara slips and once more I'm scrabbling to hold on to her. My anger explodes like a hungry zemlja bursting from the ground.

Whirling around I roar, spread my wings, and lash my tail side to side forcing the humans back. My rage finds focus in Gershom. He blanches as I lock on to him and march forward, shifting Amara to one arm to reach for my lochaber.

A strong grip on my shoulder stops my forward motion and I whirl. Sverre meets my gaze. He grabs the arm that is reaching for my weapon and shakes his head. He doesn't force me, instead he appeals to reason. It pierces through the cloud of my anger, finding me in the tempest of emotions and pulling me up to a more reasoned state.

"Let me go," I say, my voice soft.

"You know I cannot do that."

"She needs help," I hiss.

"Then let's help her."

I look at Amara in my arm and the fury fades as fast as it came. She is what matters.

Three humans come closer, moving tentatively. Sverre motions to them and they reach out for Amara. Instinct screams at me to not let them take her away. I push that aside. They're here to help. There is nothing I can do for her. That realization hits me like a punch to the stomach. I can't help her. She is mine, my treasure, and helping her is beyond any skills I have.

My wings fold in as the humans take her and then rush off. I let my tail fall to the ground as a weight settles onto my shoulders so heavy I don't know if I can even continue to stand. I've never felt so helpless in my life. Sverre moves closer and puts an arm around my shoulders. I'm staring at the ground as I try to accept the situation. Rosalind's white boots step into my line of vision so I look up and meet her eyes. There is a kindness in them I have never seen before.

"Where's Mark?" Gershom yells from behind me.

The crowd murmurs then takes up the question. They push forward, surrounding the three of us. I look them over. They're scared but they're also dirty and angry.

"Shidan, what happened?" Rosalind asks.

"There was nothing left to the box but there were pipes leading off into the distance. We were trying to find where they led," I answer, shrugging and staring off in the direction they took Amara.

"What happened Shidan? Where is the other human?" Sverre asks.

I look at him. Gershom stands behind with his arms crossed, glaring at me.

"He killed him!" Gershom yells. The crowd gasps and then everyone is talking at once. "I said this would happen. No one wanted to believe me but I knew! You can't trust these aliens!"

"Everyone calm down!" Rosalind yells, but the crowd is becoming ugly.

Shouts flare up as they push in closer. They're yelling, someone calls out murderer and then something flies from the group and hits me in the head. Pain flashes. My vision turns red, my hands ball into fists and my tail moves into a fighting position.

71

They're pushing in and I will have to take them all out. They took Amara. Pain and anger mix and then the fog of the past covers my thoughts. There is nothing but survival. Everyone outside of me is an enemy. They've taken Amara away.

Spreading my wings I scream my anger at the betrayal. Gershom is in my line of sight and I head for him. Sverre appears in my face but I'll tear him apart if I have to, anything to get to Amara. He is just another barrier. Nothing will stop me from reaching her.

"SHIDAN!" Sverre yells into my face, gripping me by both shoulders. "Amara would not want this."

Something in his voice cuts through the bijass' fog. He's right. I know he's right. I have to be better than this. I am not the animal. I am in control.

"MURDERER!" someone yells from the crowd.

Sverre pulls me away. Rosalind is in front of me again.

"Shidan, what happened? Tell me the story," she says. "Please."

I tell her what happened. I leave nothing out. It is my fault. I should not have let the humans get so far away from me. My mistake almost cost Amara her life. I was stupid. I put her in this situation. If I'd seen the ioza before they got close we could have avoided everything.

"There was nothing you could do to save Mark?" Rosalind asks.

"No," I say.

She nods then glances over and motions at Gershom. He comes closer with a tentative step, keeping an eye on me. She relates the story to him and it's obvious that Gershom doesn't believe it.

"He's lying," Gershom says, glaring at me but behind that glare is a grin.

"I doubt that," Rosalind says.

"You buy into their lies. I don't. He saved the woman, why? Because that's the one he wants to mate with. He's no different from these others. He's after our women. I'm not surprised at all that Mark didn't return."

"Then why did you suggest he go? Why send a man to his death if you were so sure?" Rosalind asks.

"I didn't send him to his death. A suspicion is not fact. Even now there is a hint of doubt, isn't there? I could be wrong," Gershom says, dancing all around the truth of what he means.

He's a zmeya, a sand snake that strikes when you least expect. I'll deal with him, not here, not now, but soon. He's a hidden threat and I don't know why Rosalind and the others don't see it.

"It was an accident," Rosalind answers. "This world is dangerous. Mark knew the risks when he left."

"You would say that," Gershom says.

"Where is Ladon?" I ask Sverre.

"He is with Calista, she is not being allowed out of bed," Sverre says.

The motions of his tail, the rustle of his wings, and the green tinge to the edge of his scales shows he's worried.

"How bad is it?" I ask and Sverre shakes his head in response. "Jolie?"

Again he shakes his head but his concern is obvious. "She's fine, so far," he says. "We do not know. There are too many questions and no answers."

"Where have they taken Amara?"

"I will take you," he says, leading us away from the crowd of still arguing humans. Let them. None of them matter like Amara does. They can accept the truth or not as they like. I will not waste my time trying to convince them.

7

AMARA

"*W*hat did you do!" I scream, jerking awake.

The moment my eyes open I know I'm back. It's all gone. The ship, my home is no more. My fighter, gone. I've lost everything that ever mattered and I'm here, in hell, with nothing left.

Again.

I defined my life by that fighter. I was the best. No one could deny it no matter how they tried. Here, I'm a two-bit engineer. It doesn't matter that I know jack all about engineering. I know how to put a fighter together, which translates to knowing nothing as far as what we need here. There are no fighters to fly or maintain. There's nothing here but a big, empty, hell-hole desert. Fuck Tatooine, fuck Vulcan, fuck this place!

"Lyutik, calm dow-"

"No!" I scream, cutting him off. "And quit calling me that!"

Shidan holds his hands up.

It's his fault, it has to be. Everything is foggy, it's hard to think. It was fine, I was back on the ship and happy but he couldn't be okay with that. He pulled me back here. He wants me to be his damn treasure but I want what I had.

"Damn you Zmaj and your treasures. I'm no one's treasure! I don't need help, I don't need you!"

"Amara," he says, backing away from me.

I look for something to throw at him. "It's your fault!"

"What is?"

"That I'm here! I'm back here, I was there and everything was back to normal. I was about to show up that son of a bitch Draker. I would have beat him hands down! Then they'd all respect me. They'd know I didn't have help. I worked hard, I earned those damn wings!"

"Yes Amara but you don't understand. That wasn't real it was just a-"

"It was too! Damn it, it was real!"

Emotions whirl through me. Shidan shakes his head. Storming forward, rage pulses through every muscle of my body. I was happy. Things were how they're supposed to be. My life made sense. Shidan retreats until his back is against the wall. I press close enough I have to strain my head back to glare at him.

"Amara, the ioza plant, it makes you see hallucinations so you won't fight it, it-"

"No, it was… real. I would have beat him!"

Doubt tears at the edges of my certainty.

"Lyutik-"

I swing without thinking, cutting off his words but Shidan grabs my wrist. We're staring into each other's eyes. I swing with my free hand and he grabs it too. Holding me tight he spins us around and presses me against the wall. His massive, strong body crushes me, holding me in place. Staring into his eyes, certainty falls to pieces. Our lips meet with intense force. Fire rages to life in my core. Desire awakens in a blaze I can't control.

He holds my wrists with bruising force. His lips against mine, moving, I resist… at first. Struggling in his grip, I push against him but he's big, strong, and in control. I want to escape but I don't. His lips are exotic, tasting of hints of spice. His tongue pushes its way into my mouth, an invader, and despite everything I open myself. My tongue rises to meet his almost like it has a will of its own.

His huge, overly muscled body presses against me, his erection presses hard into my belly. Heat, clenching need and wetness burn between my legs. I lose myself in his kiss, in the pressure of his hard body against mine. My sensitive nipples crush between us as we wrestle for control.

He shifts his grip, taking both my wrists in one hand, holding them over my head. My shoulders scream in discomfort but it only adds fuel to the fire of my desire. With one hand free, he grabs my ass and lowers his hips, pressing what feels like an impossibly large hardness onto my clit through my clothes. Involuntarily I grind against it, desire, need, and pure lust taking control. Our tongues work against each other, fighting for dominance over the kiss. His lips claim me and in that moment I am his. Helpless, he's in control.

Then I remember what happens when someone gets too close.

"No," I push back.

He breaks the kiss and we stare into each other's eyes. His confusion is obvious. I want to pull him in close but I can't. I won't. I'm not the one for him, he deserves better.

"Amara?" he asks.

"Get out," I say, my voice hoarse.

Internal conflict rages but I can't. He lets go of my wrists but remains close. His head tilts to one side and every part of me wants him to take me but I can't let that happen. Tears fall down my cheeks, emotions too strong to handle rage, choking me. I can't breathe. Space. I need space.

"GET OUT!" I scream.

He steps back and I see the pain in his eyes. He's confused, hurt, and it's all my fault and damn it I can't do anything about it.

Anger surges out of the burning fires of desire and I lose it. I push against his chest and connecting with the solid, muscled mass of him feels good so I do it again. I scream and he backs up, stepping away with each shove. I push until he's out the door then I slam it shut. Turning, I lean against it and slide to the floor, tears streaming down my face.

"I won't let anyone else get hurt," I whisper, trying to convince myself.

Climbing to my feet, I rinse my face in a bowl of water then go to my bunk. I slip out of my clothes and under the salvaged blanket, staring at the ceiling. His lips were soft. So much softer than I expected. And that flavor, exotic, enticing awakened a long buried and forgotten need. An itch I haven't scratched in a long time, even before the wreck and destruction of my entire world.

My nipples stiffen at the memory of Shidan's strong hands holding me. In that instant I knew I was helpless. I hated it, but then something in me reacted different. Part of me liked it. I could have let him have it. Let him be in control but I had to fight it. He could handle it. The rough cloth of my blanket shifts across the diamond points of my nipples sending a shudder down my spine.

I cover the left with my hand to protect it and heat flares in my breast at my touch. The memory of his body pressing hard against mine consumes my thoughts. The way he felt, his erection digging into my stomach. He felt huge, massive, and now I'm wondering what his cock looks like. What would it feel like if I let him slide it into me?

My free hand drifts down between my thighs. I'm soaking wet with desire. Using a light pressure I rub a slow circle over my clitoris while my other hand pinches my nipple making it even harder.

He's strong. I like that. He took control, and he took what he wanted and it felt so damn good. My fingers slide inside. My back arches as I enter myself. I imagine it being him. Pinning me down, he slides into me. Fills me with his massive cock. My pussy spreads to take him in. Pushing my fingers in and out as I think of him entering me, my core tightens. My fingers graze my clit. My back arches as muscles clench. His spicy, exotic lips claim mine. The bruises on my wrists, the ache in my shoulders as he holds my hands over my head. The way he'd take me, make me his.

I fuck myself faster. My fingers drive in and out as my wetness covers them. Three fingers slide in.

Imagination takes over. He's lifts me up by my wrists and carries me to the bed by hooking a hand under my ass. He squeezes my cheeks pulling my ass open as one of his rough fingers caresses my wetness. My delicate lips part before his touch.

A shudder races through my body. Spreading my fingers I fill myself up and drag them out and up over my clit. Pinching my nipple with my free hand I tug and pull on it as my fingers move faster. The pressure in my core is building. I'm gasping in air as my desire winds tighter.

Throwing me on the bed he leans over. His larger size engulfs me as he lowers himself between my legs. His tongue is rough as he drags along my opening, tasting my sweet wetness. He drives his tongue through my silken folds and I'm carried away to a new place.

My fingers explore as I dream of his tongue. He's dominating but attentive, I know he will be. The attention to detail he shows when he thinks he's caring for me make him an amazing lover. As my core tightens, I can't wait any longer.

His massive cock pushes into my opening. He's big, bigger than anything I've ever had. He slides in slowly, letting me get used to his girth. Nerves alight, everything is on fire. My mind explodes as I'm driven over the edge. Every muscle tightens and knots up, my toes curl and I can't breathe. Awareness returns in a slow pass back to reality as I collapse on the bed and exhaustion hits me.

I shouldn't have kicked him out.

No, I did the right thing.

8

SHIDAN

*A*s I storm out of Amara's building, bijass fog clouds my thoughts. The urge to claim what's mine beats with every pulse of my hearts. I fight against it but I'm holding on by the tips of my fingers. It's primal and instinctual and so strong I have to get away.

Her lips were soft on mine and tasted sweet, like a delicate fruit that lingers on my tongue. My cock stiffens as the memory of her body pressing against mine consumes me. Leaving her is the hardest thing I've done in my life and the bijass rises, vying for control. Why does she fight me? Why do I not just take her, make her mine?

Heat flushes through my limbs. My cock throbs. As I step out into the night, rage is just a breath away. I want to destroy something. Anything. I want to take what's mine. The bijass demands it. Defend my territory. Destroy any that dare stand against me.

My muscles twitch, my hands ball into tight fists. I need a target. Something to focus my anger on but the street is empty. Pacing up and down it I see the ravages of time. The destruction that eats away at what was once a part of a great civilization. Sverre talks of it. Ladon does too. I don't remember it. My world before Amara was only me, surviving. Alone. The way it should be. What could be greater than me against the world?

It was a mistake to stay here. That's what is wrong. I've heard the tale of Sverre and of Ladon. They took their women and kept them alone, at least for a time. If I took Amara with me to my home, showed her how life could be if it was just the two of us then she'd see.

The glimmer of a plan forms in the fog. My home is nice. I can provide for her there. Make her feel welcome, protect her. Take her away from these others. They are the ones who make her feel she has to be strong. They put it on her, refusing to treat her as a treasure should be. Out there, in the desert where my home is, she would see how life can be.

This is no home. An empty shell of a memory. No comforts, no care, slowly dying while everyone argues and debates. These humans have time to hate because they don't know what it takes to survive. I know what it takes. I've survived, it's all I know. Great civilization. Who needs it? It did nothing for me. What I have, what I know, I've learned on my own. I tried listening to Sverre. He's an elder and supposed to be wise but his words have not helped.

Amara pushed me away. She stopped what she started. I didn't start it, she did. I can still feel the press of her soft mounds against my chest and now I desperately want to hold them in my hands. I could feel her heart beating. Her tongue, both rough and soft, the sweet taste of her lips. My prime penis pounds with need, demanding relief.

I will do it, take her away and show her how it can be. It's the only answer.

Turning on my heel, I about-face and move back the way I came, but rounding the corner I stop in my tracks. Astarot approaches down the street. Rage erupts from deep inside and I see red. Astarot showed up here at the same time I did and we fought over Amara when I first saw her. I know he's not my equal in combat. I should have finished him that day but Sverre stopped me.

He walks with a swagger, his tail moving side to side, his wings rustling. He's after her again. I'm certain of it. No Zmaj walks that way unless he's looking to mate. The bright blue tinge on his scales screams for females to look at him. He's after my female. He thinks to show me up?

Bursting into a run, I spread my wings as I get close and leap. I cock my fist as I come down and strike him across the face. He isn't ready for my attack. As I hit him, his head slams to one side, and he stumbles, dropping to one knee. I don't give him an opportunity to regroup. I hit him with my other hand then swing my tail around and slam it into his ribs with devastating force.

"Leave her be!" I scream. "She's mine!"

Blood drips from his mouth. He looks up at me and grins, then his tail swings around and slams into my legs. I'm almost knocked off my feet. Stumbling backwards until there is distance between us, I regain my balance and drop into a defensive stance.

"Going to teach you a lesson infant," Astarot says.

"Try me," I hiss.

He lunges. I drop low and swing up as he comes in, hitting him in the gut. His air whoofs out as I rise into the punch, lifting him off the ground. He spreads his wings trying to roll with the hit. I swing my tail up and over my head, slamming it down on his head. It's a stunning move. I know he'll be seeing stars after that blow. He drops to the ground and rolls away as I try to stomp him.

He comes to his feet in a low crouch. Raging, I storm forward, unwilling to yield an inch. I know he's here for Amara. He wants her. He wanted her when we arrived. How could anyone not want her? She's perfect, beautiful, and stunning. I see through his machinations. I won't let him get close to her.

"Nice punch," he says.

"Stay away from her."

"Who?"

He's pretending ignorance, treating me like a fool which makes me even angrier. Like I can't see the truth! We circle each other, looking for an opening. Any sign of weakness. I jab and feint, probing his defenses. He bobs and weaves. His wings spread part-way and back, creating a distraction, an illusion to fool they eye and make it harder to see where his hands are. It's a trick any young male knows. It also distracts your opponent from your tail, the single most deadly weapon a Zmaj has.

"Who are we talking about?" he asks again. "Come on Shidan, talk."

"Amara," I hiss.

"Oh, her?" He seems surprised.

"Of course her!" I scream, lunging forward.

He dodges to the side as I grab. I catch his arm, spinning him around as I move through where he was standing. Jerking him in close, we're face to face. I glare into his dark eyes.

"I'm not here for her," he says. "You're in the bijass. Fight it."

I punch him in the gut again with my free hand while holding him close so he can't roll with it. His eyes widen in shock as the air rushes out of his lungs.

"You can't have her!" I scream, pulling him up straight as he tries to double over.

I slam him against the wall of the building, cracking his head.

"Fine." He shakes his head to clear it. "I don't want her."

"Liar!"

"No Shidan. Damn it think. Clear your head, push past the instincts."

I try. Part of me knows he's speaking truth. I'm standing in the middle of a raging storm. I struggle to remember my name. The only certain thing is Amara. She is my rock. The thought of her calms me and the fog recedes as my rage disappears as fast as it came.

"You can't have her," I say, but the conviction is fading.

"I don't want her." He grips me by my shoulders, pushing back until I'm at arm's length.

He doesn't want her. How could this be true? He must feel the depths of my desire.

"Why are you here?" I ask, suspicious, but the storm inside is calming, the fog receding.

"Here where?" he asks. "I'm heading for the main square to, uh, talk with Rosalind," he smiles and the scales of his face lighten in color.

Staring at him I search for any hint of a lie. There's something but I don't think it involves Amara. At last I step back.

"Okay," I say, rolling my shoulders and working the knots out.

Astarot cocks his head to one side, rubbing his jaw. He's breathing heavy and blood trickles from the corner of his mouth. His dark eyes stare until I feel uncomfortable which makes me want to hit him again.

"She's the one huh?" he asks.

I look away rather than answer. He grunts then places an arm around my shoulders.

"I understand," he says. "How old are you Shidan?"

I shrug his arm off and step away. "What does it matter?"

He moves up and walks next to me, uninvited and unwelcome. Rather than start another fight I ignore him.

"Well it matters a lot," he says. "See, if you are as young as

I think you are, you were what, not even in adulthood when the devastation hit?"

I glance at him over my shoulder and he nods as if I told him everything he needed to know.

"Yeah, thought so."

"Why don't you leave me alone?" I demand.

"Because right now you need a friend," he says. "And I like pushing the limits. You think I don't feel the urge to take you out? Trust me, I do. I want to fight every other male I see but rather than give in to it, I push it. I tempt myself, put myself in situations where I have to face it head on. Sooner or later I'll master it and then it won't bother me any longer."

"You're insane," I say.

He shrugs and smiles. "Maybe."

"Go away."

"Yeah, can't do that."

Every fiber of me wants to hit him hard enough to break that smile, so he never uses it again. The urge is strong enough that a shudder runs down my spine and my hands convulse into fists. Glancing at him over my shoulder, he walks with a swagger and confidence that rubs me wrong. The urge to destroy him bubbles below the surface of my control, ready to boil over into rage.

"What do you want?" I ask.

"Good question," he says, and looks like he gives it some serious thought before continuing. "Well, you lost yourself to the bijass, that much is obvious. I guess I want to help."

"I don't need your help."

"Sure," he says. "But I'm giving it anyway, just the kind of guy I am I guess."

"Annoying?"

"That too," he agrees. "It didn't use to be this way. Do you remember?"

"No."

"Yeah, didn't think so. It wasn't so hard before. Also, when you feel the calling— well if the girl was a Zmaj she'd feel it too, so that made things much easier. These… humans, they're different."

He shakes his head and we walk in silence. I wait for him to speak again but he seems content to say nothing. At last the silence pushes me.

"What about them?" I ask.

"Hm?"

"The humans, how are they different?"

"Oh, right? They're so… enticing, aren't they?"

My irritation with him grows again, causing my tail to shift back and forth faster. "Do you have a point?"

"Sure," he says.

"What is it!" Exasperation makes me yell.

"Be able to bend."

"Bend what?"

"Yourself," he replies.

"You make no sense."

"Sure I do, you just don't want to hear it yet. You'll get it, think about it. Be flexible. These aren't Zmaj women now are they? They're different, exotic, special even. If you're rigid, fixed in your ways and ideas, then you'll get nowhere."

"And now you're an expert on the humans?" I ask, mocking.

"Nothing like that, I'm just an observer," he says, ignoring my tone.

"I think I could come to hate you."

"Yeah, I get that a lot." He smiles then turns and walks off towards the town center.

Bend.

Whatever, he's as crazy as a bivo drugged on koren root.

9

AMARA

I screwed up. I shouldn't have let things go so far with Shidan. Now he's being weird or maybe it's me. I don't know. What I do know is that now things are uncomfortable. He annoyed me before with his always being there, hovering, bumping into me every time I turn around but now it's like we can't meet each other's eyes. Every time we do, he or I look away. Like we have some dirty secret we don't want to admit to the world.

Butterflies dance in my stomach and it takes a while for me to realize its nervousness. My skin tingles, the hair on my arms stands on end, and everything seems loud. At random moments the room will close in on me. There's not enough air, Shidan's presence fills the space. I can't find any place to look that I'm not seeing him.

"All right, we need a solution," Rosalind says from the head of the table.

Focus on her. I'll take any distraction I can get. Something has to work. Anything to keep my mind off of Shidan. The taste of his lips, the feel of his body against mine... focus!

"How bad is it?" Mei asks.

I can't help but notice Shidan looking at her and on top of the firestorm of emotions raging inside me there is a sharp, stabbing pain straight into my chest. Looking from him to her then back again, the look on his face pisses me off. I'm so angry I can't stand it. He shouldn't be looking at her like that!

"It's... bad," Jolie says, leaning back in her chair, very pregnant herself. "Calista is on strict bed rest and that seems to help. The problem is we don't understand what's going on. The interaction between our two species, the differences between Zmaj female anatomy and our own. We're working off of guesses and hoping that nature will take its course."

"Except nothing about this is natural," Gershom says.

Why is he even here? I think, rolling my eyes and resisting the urge to speak. At least he's a suitable distraction.

"That is not helpful," Rosalind says.

Gershom nods and shuts his mouth. Something passes between him and Rosalind and I have to wonder what's going on there.

"How's Ladon?" I ask.

The look everyone at the table exchanges says it all. The elephant in the room is Ladon, Calista's lover. While the Zmaj have had a hard time with learning to be social, since Calista's difficulties Ladon has been worse, or at least that's what I've heard. I haven't seen him in a few days.

"We need to figure this out," Rosalind says.

"That bad, huh?" I ask.

"Yes," she says.

"Shoot me straight, how bad?" I ask Sverre.

Sverre looks down at the table, staring intently while his fingers trace a pattern. When he looks up, he meets my eyes and everything I need to know is right there. It's bad. Worse than bad.

"It is grim," he says.

I nod. "So do we have any ideas?"

"Since your expedition didn't pan out— " Rosalind starts.

"And Mark died," Gershom interrupts.

"Yes and we lost Mark, limiting our options," she finishes.

Silence falls across the room. Most everyone stares at the table in front of them. Looking around, I see each of my friends. Rosalind, imperial and strong standing at the head. Sverre stands next to her. Seated to his right is Jolie, her hand resting on her pregnant belly. It's obvious she's worried what will happen with her and her own baby when her pregnancy reaches the stage that Calista's in, which can't be that far away. Inga sits next to Jolie, silent and overwhelmed, tears shine in the corners of her eyes. Beautiful Mei is sitting next to me, tapping her fingers on the table. Shidan is on the far side of her, also next to Rosalind.

Gershom is the only one present who I don't consider a friend. He's a douche, so he doesn't count. I bet he's a Star Trek Enterprise fan. He would be, dick head. Everyone knows it's the worst of the Star Trek series, Scott Bakula should have kept making Quantum Leap.

"So we're screwed? Just hope it all comes out okay?" I ask, irritation rising.

I don't leave things to hope, assess risks and act. That's what I do. There has to be a better way.

"Maybe not," Rosalind replies.

"What?" I ask.

She bites her lower lip and hesitates then nods to herself. "The ship," she says.

"What about the ship?" I ask as everyone at the table looks at her confused.

"It might contain something that will help."

"Like what? I thought we scavenged what was worth saving off of it," I say, and a murmur of agreement goes around the table.

"No," she says. "We took what was necessary to survive."

"Right, like I said…"

"At that time," she adds.

It hits me like a light going on in a dark room. "There might be tech, we took nothing like that!"

"Yes," Rosalind says. "The Infantry medical bay was in the section of the ship we crashed in. There is military tech that could be helpful."

"What about powering it?" I ask.

"I'm counting on you for that," she says. "There were small generators and the Medical Unit had self-sustained power. The condition of that tech or the viability of moving it is your area."

"If there's a small core generator that would help with our power issues. At least enough to power any medical equipment," I muse.

"That would make sense," Rosalind agrees.

"Hm, it could be bad though," I say as I think it through.

"What do you mean?" Inga asks.

"If there is a small core, great, we have a power source, but if there is damage to the core we're screwed."

"So nothing to lose right? Either it's working, or it's not, right?" Mei asks.

"Actually, a lot to lose. If it's damaged, it will leak radiation. The area will be a death trap."

"Oh," Mei says.

"Yeah, that's the bad," I say.

Rosalind bows her head and her shoulders slump. The weight of the decision is on her and we all know it. It's not a job she asked for and I know that too. We follow her because she is who she is. Before the crash I only knew her by reputation. I would see her at dress parades or inspections on rare occasions but it's not like the Lady General and I traveled in the same social circles. It's a moment, a short one, then she looks up and meets the eyes of every person at the table.

"This is the only option we have," she says. "We have to take it."

"Fine. I'm going," I say.

"I'm going too," Shidan jumps in.

I glare at him but it doesn't phase him. He meets my glare, crossing his arms over his chest and lifting his chin so he's staring down his nose at me.

"We can't send our only engineer," Jolie says.

"I'm the only one that has a chance in hell of knowing what I'm looking for," I answer her.

"She's right, even though I don't like it either," Rosalind says.

"We should send a team, a *human* team. They could then bring back other necessary supplies," Gershom adds.

Jolie looks from me to Rosalind trying to find an argument. Rosalind focuses on Gershom and his idiocy. I lock eyes with Jolie, smile, then whisper to her.

"It's fine," I mouth.

She shakes her head, emphatic.

"Gershom," Rosalind says over the top of Jolie and I's private conversation. "This mission requires stealth. A large contingent will attract attention. We don't know if the pirates are still out there or not."

"Fine, but I still want someone I know is loyal to us to go," Gershom says, adamantly stubborn.

"Because that worked out so well last time?" I throw out, thinking of poor Mark.

Jolie is mouthing no at me over and over while shaking her head. We're going back and forth in a war of silent words. She glances at Gershom and arches an eyebrow then looks back at me, showing I should let him send some of his people. I would, god knows I'd be glad to let him go burn in the sand, but this mission is too important.

Calista's life is at stake. Her baby's life too. And Jolie and her baby. No, I have to do this. I'm the only one with the knowledge to come back with what we need. Those idiots would come back with a load of vid sticks and nothing of any actual use.

"Amara is going and I am too, it's the only way. There is nothing more to say," Shidan says from behind me and I jump in surprise.

I hadn't realized he'd come closer. Glancing up at him towering over me, he's glaring at Jolie with his arms still crossed. Jolie's mouth drops open and her eyes widen at him inserting himself into our argument. It makes me frown too.

"Who asked for your input," I grouse.

He's being more forceful than normal, assertive, in control and decisive. He glances down at me, I don't think I'd stop him if he grabbed me up in his arms and kissed me here in front of everyone. Maybe. Or I would, but the ache deep in my core wants him to, even if I would try to stop him.

The moment passes. His gaze returns to Jolie, implacable. Only then do I realize that every eye at the table is on us. Rosalind is leaning on the table glaring at Shidan. He stares straight ahead, ignoring everyone.

"What in the hell did he say?" Gershom asks.

"He agreed with me," Rosalind says. "He doesn't want a repeat of Mark."

I'm surprised she would add that to what Shidan said, but it hits Gershom hard. His eyes widen, his mouth moves then snaps shut.

"Fine," he says with a sharp nod.

Maybe he does care about his people? No, I doubt it, it's all a show and a power grab for him. If Gershom grows a heart, then I'll fall head over heels in love with Shidan. It's just something that can't be. I can't open myself up that way and Gershom can't get past his power hunger.

"It's settled then," Rosalind says.

Jolie's upset is apparent on her face. Tears well in the corners of her eyes as she stands, shakes her head, then walks over to stand next to Sverre. She holds on to his arm while staring at the floor. The others stand and head out of the room, leaving only Sverre, Jolie, Shidan, Gershom, Rosalind and myself.

"I don't like this," Gershom says.

"Of course you don't," Rosalind quips.

"You can make fun of me all you want to but you don't see what I see. I'm right and sooner or later you will regret your decisions. One day you will look back and say I was right."

"I'm sure you'll be there to gloat when I do," Rosalind says.

"It's not about that," he says, glaring at Jolie's pregnant stomach. "Not at all."

He turns and walks out of the room and a cloud lifts. His presence is irritating, and it's a relief when he's gone.

"I do not know where the ship crashed," Shidan says. "I found the city first."

"I can give you directions," Sverre says.

"Good, we'll need supplies," Shidan says.

"Who the hell put you in charge?" I ask, stepping up beside him and inserting myself into the conversation.

Shidan looks angry but I don't care. He can get happy in the same boots he got mad in. I'm not letting him take control without me having my input.

"Okay," he says, snapping his mouth shut.

"And don't you forget it," I say.

Sverre watches the two of us bantering back and forth but adds nothing to the conversation. Smart. Jolie stares at the floor, still displaying her displeasure with silence. Rosalind crosses her arms.

"If the bickering is over, we need to organize this expedition. You'll need supplies like Shidan said, it's a couple days to the ship then there will be a trip back. You'll need food, water, vitamin supplements, and a supply of epis to make sure you don't go past your dosage. Even then it only lasts a week at the most, you'll have to be quick."

"It will last less than a few days outside the dome," Sverre says.

"Yeah, yeah, I know," I say.

"Do you?" Sverre asks, glancing at Jolie. "In the city, even before the dome was working, you had shelter. Out there you won't. The drain on your human body will be a thousand times what you've experienced and it won't stop."

"I get it," I say, but Sverre shakes his head. "I was just out there."

"I almost lost Jolie out there," he says.

"I know," I say, brushing aside his concerns. Stressing things I can't do anything about gets us nowhere. "Let's get on with it."

Sverre shakes his head but says nothing else. The small group of us leave the meeting room and go to the supply center. An older man I don't know is on duty.

"Bert," Rosalind greets him as we walk in.

"Lady General," Bert says.

He's wearing a dirty, gray security guard uniform complete with a stunner on his side. He has a clipboard in his hand and stands stiffly.

"At ease," Rosalind says. "I keep telling you you're not enlisted Bert."

"Yes Ma'am," he replies.

"We're sending two people out on a mission," Rosalind says. "I need them supplied. Make sure they have epis."

"Our supplies are low, Ma'am," he replies.

Rosalind grimaces then nods. "I know."

Bert leads us through a set of double doors into a room that's filled with shelving. It hits me how empty most of these shelves are. My stomach grumbles, less in hunger I think than in anticipation and worry of running out of food. Apparently Rosalind keeps this quiet because I had no idea it was this bad. The situation is more grim than anyone knows.

"Damn," I exhale and Rosalind looks at me sharply.

I shrug. What does she expect? It's more than obvious we're screwed in the not so distant future. Food, medicine, and basic survival supplies are running low. Either we fix it soon or, or what? We fix it that's it. There's no other option.

Bert leads us through the empty rows of shelving and into a corner. There's a large refrigerator chest we brought from the wrecked ship. He's still using it despite the lack of power to cool it which makes sense. It's good for storage and air tight so it will keep out anything foreign. He opens the chest, pulls out a package wrapped in leather skins. Placing it on an empty shelf he unwraps it to reveal sliced pieces of smoked meat. He gathers some of these and transfers them to another piece of similar looking leather. Once he's done, he wraps both of them and returns the larger package to the chest.

"Thanks," I say, taking the offered food.

"No problem," he says. "You'll need vitamin packs. They're over here."

It doesn't take long before we're outfitted the best we can be. Outside the dome the world is, well I've thought it before, it's hell. It's not Vulcan or Tatooine, it's hell straight out of Dante's Inferno or something.

We leave Bert behind and emerge back into the bright light of the outside. The supply center is close to the town center where the old fountain is. Standing in the big open space and looking up, I can see the suns are setting by the length of the shadows.

"You should try to sleep," Rosalind says.

"I'd rather just go," I reply.

"That is not wise," Shidan inserts.

"How is it not? The sun will bake the hell out of us. At least if we travel at night it won't be as hot," I say.

"Sismis hunt at night for one," he says.

"What the hell is a sismis?" I ask.

"Flying flesh hunters," he adds, not helpful at all so I roll my eyes. "They hunt in packs and are not afraid to attack us."

"And?" I ask in a mocking tone. "What else you got?"

"He's right," Rosalind says.

"Why are you taking his side?"

"Because he's right," she repeats.

I cross my arms over my chest and dig in my heels. I don't care if he's right, I don't want to be out there in the daylight. I'd rather travel at night when it's cooler.

"If I travel at night, the heat won't be as bad. I'll be able to go faster," I say.

"Speaking of which, make sure you take your epis. Every two days, three at the most. Every day after that it loses potency and your body will go into withdrawal. It's vital you get there and back fast," Rosalind adds.

"Yeah, yeah," I say. "Let's go."

Rosalind shrugs so I look at Shidan.

"It is not wise," he says.

"You wanted in on this so let's go. Now. Faster we go the faster we get home," I say.

He considers it then nods his agreement.

"Best of luck," Rosalind says.

"Thanks," I reply.

"If you can carry them, bring back vid sticks," she says.

"You're kidding me," I say in surprise. I wouldn't have expected her to have any interest in ancient pop culture movies.

"No, I'm not. We have nothing here to entertain the masses. It's leaving them with too much time to think."

"Ah, I get it."

She smiles weakly then walks away. Shidan and I look at each other. I heft my backpack up higher on my shoulders and motion with my head. He nods and we walk.

At least I got my way on one thing.

10

SHIDAN

*I*t's dark but Amara insists we keep moving.

"We should rest," I say.

"We'll rest when we get there," she barks.

She's struggling to climb the dune. Sand slips with each step she takes so each step forward is half a step back. Reaching out, I grab her by the arms, flap my wings and lift, carrying her to the top of the dune. She struggles the entire way, kicking me in my shins and shifting her weight side to side. It's twice as hard as it should be. I set her down on the top of the dune and stare.

"Let me go! You and your damn big muscles and wings and gah!" She turns towards me then pounds her hands against my chest. "Ouch! Why do you have to have so many damn muscles!"

I shake my head. I don't know what she's doing or why she's acting this way. The worst part? It makes me want her. The more she resists me, the more beautiful she seems. My cock jumps, pulsing with wanting her. In some weird, twisted way, it's a display of her strength. Underneath the outbursts, she wants me. I know she does. The memory of her lips on mine, the softness of her body pressing against me... my prime penis stiffens, announcing my desire to the world. I turn away, embarrassed that even her anger arouses me.

"You needed help," I say over my shoulder.

I know it was the wrong thing to say. Her eyes widen and her mouth tightens to a hard line.

"I did NOT need your help," she says. "I was making it fine on my own before you got involved!"

I know I won't win so I nod and point off into the distance. Hands on hips, she stares, waiting for me to say something more. Only when I don't does she come to stand beside me. She's close. So close we're almost touching yet we aren't. The tiny amount of space between us pulls my attention and holds it. It's like I'm staring across a vast, empty gulf. I want her to touch my scales, I want to press myself against her, trace her soft curves with my fingers. Lost in my fantasy I miss her words.

"Huh?" I ask, jerking my mind back to the moment.

"I said how much farther do you think it is?" she asks, irritation in her voice.

There is a small twitch between her eyes where she frowns. Of their own accord my arms reach for her but I stop them, forcing them back to my sides. Her arms are crossed over her chest and accent her soft mounds. The loose cloth she wears pulls back in a gentle, hot breeze. My cock pulses, pounding a rhythm of its own creation, singing of desire and need.

"I don't know," I answer, but my voice is hoarse and harsh to my ears.

My fingers twitch as I struggle to regain control. She stares and the primal fog rises, clouding my thoughts. Her ass, so soft, should be in my hands. I want her lips against mine. What does she look like under those layers? I've imagined it so many times but I know my fantasies will pale to the reality of her.

"Great," she mutters, turning away.

I'm left in darkness, alone, weak and trembling from having stood too long in the beauty of her gaze. Like a mewling newborn and realizing it, anger rushes in. I'm no newborn, I'm strong, I will show her what kind of man I am and I will care for her whether she wants it or not. A treasure does not get to choose to not be what it is. She is mine and sooner or later she will know.

"It will be even longer if you don't let me help you," I hiss.

She whirls on me, fury plain on her face. Her small hands ball into fists and her eyes flash.

"I don't NEED your help!" she screams.

My anger is white hot but before I can express it, something behind her flashes, catching my eye. An instant and it's gone. I react without thinking, grabbing and spinning her so her back is against my chest as I twist and drop to the ground on my side, shielding her from the impact.

"What are you doing— "

I cut her off by putting my hand over her mouth. She fights against me with all she has. Her breath is sharp and fast through her nose. I roll so I'm on top of her then use my tail to shift the sand, digging us down in. Shifting my wings, the sand pours in over us until we're partially covered. She's still struggling which will ruin the disguise.

"Stop," I hiss. "Pirates!"

I speak softly and she stops struggling. She tilts her head up and our eyes meet. Only once I'm sure she will not scream any more do I remove my hand from her mouth.

"You're sure?" she asks in a whisper.

I nod. I feel her heart pounding in her chest against me. In a flash of embarrassment I realize my body is responding to her closeness. My cock is rock hard, pressing against her backside. I focus my attention towards where I saw the pirates, hoping it will stop. She shifts beneath me, trying to get more comfortable. I don't know if it makes her more comfortable, but it pulls my attention right back where I don't want it. I almost lose myself as she rotates her hips.

A metal clang a short distance away resounds across the sand and we both go stock still. Her breathing slows but her heart continues to pound wildly. Staring ahead and down the dune, dark shapes are moving around. Did they spot us? Time slows to a crawl. There's an eternity between each beating of my hearts as I watch the figures below. There are three, maybe four. They're walking in a loose formation across the desert. All are well-armed and equipped. They stop and gather into a huddle.

This is it. If they spotted us, I'll know in a moment. Tactics race through my mind as I play out possible scenarios. I have to protect her. It doesn't matter what happens to me, they can't have her. I won't allow any harm to Amara. I consider and discard a dozen options until at last there remains only one that will accomplish my goal.

"If they attack, stay hidden," I whisper.

"No way," she whispers back. "I can help."

Anger flares. Even now, in imminent danger, she won't just listen! I want to force her to obey, somehow. My emotions are so strong it makes me shake, causing the sand to shift around us. I swallow hard as I struggle to regain control.

"Amara," I hiss. "Please, there is no other way."

We stare at each other, forgetting for a moment the danger, I lose myself in the beauty of her eyes. They remind me of when I was young and would stare up into the vast, black expanse of twinkling stars, dreaming of traveling. I would lose myself for hours, often falling asleep under the open sky.

A frown purses her lips, but she nods. I breathe a sigh of relief then put my attention back on the pirates. They're moving again, away from us and the direction we are traveling. I wait until they're well out of sight before rising and offering my hand to Amara. She stares up at it a long moment before taking it and climbing to her feet.

"Are they gone?" she asks, still speaking in a whisper.

"For the moment," I reply, staring off in the direction I saw them leave.

"Good," she says. "Don't you ever do that again!"

"Are you kidding?" I hiss, whirling on her as she glares up at me with a finger in my face.

"No, I am not kidding. You and your..." she motions with both her hands as her eyes move across my body until she's staring at the tent in my pants where my erection throbs. "Muscles and..." She trails off, still staring.

I shake my head in embarrassment but then I push the limits with her. I want her and I'm certain she wants me as much, if only she'd admit it.

"What about me?" I ask, shifting my hips so my erection points directly at her middle. I move my arms so that my biceps flex and my chest muscles ripple. My tail shifts side to side as my cock pulses.

"Don't use them... against me," she says, her voice is soft and her eyes don't leave my cock.

"Against you?" I ask, not understanding why she uses those words. Everything I do is for her, not against her.

"Yes..." she trails off.

"Perhaps you'd prefer to see what the slavers do with a beautiful woman?"

Her eyes snap up to meet mine. "Beautiful...?" Her soft, pink tongue wets her lips and she takes a half step closer.

"You heard me."

She touches my chest and heat flares, searing her touch

into my memory. My cock spasms. Our eyes lock as I lean into her touch.

"Whatever, dragon-boy," she mutters.

"I look like a boy to you?" I ask, my voice husky.

She wets her lips again and shakes her head. She swallows hard then something shifts, and she steps back. The warm spot on my chest cools, fading as her touch becomes only memory.

"Just don't do it again," she says, turning her back on me.

The moment passes. Did I do the right thing? Should I have pushed harder? Did I push too much? Damn it, so many questions. Why is everything involving her so complex?

"Fine," I hiss, anger becoming the rock I cling to in my confusion. "We should go since you're in such an all-fired hurry to get there. We still have at least a day's travel."

"Great, just what I wanted to hear," she says, hitching her pack up on to her shoulders.

We walk in silence, the moonlight illuminating our path. Amara struggles through the sand and I'm sure she's operating solely on determination and willpower. She hasn't slept since the previous night and her signs of exhaustion are unmistakable. It's a testament to her strength and yet another part of her I admire.

It's much easier for me. This is my home. My wings and tail allow me to move across the sand without being pulled down, so every step is not a struggle like it is for her. Still she refuses my help. So strong, so beautiful, so damn perfect. I'll make her mine, sooner or later.

We crest another rise. The night is receding as the suns rises, a brightening of the gloom. In the distance there are screeches from the large, vampiric, bat-like sismis returning from their nightly hunt. Except for the pirates, our first night of travel was uneventful. Amara drinks water while I take stock of our progress.

I love this planet. It's beautiful and the rising suns shows off all its glory. The first rays create sparkles across the sand. Shades of red blend towards white then back to a deep, rich color. Amara gasps next to me. She shields her eyes and looks out across the rolling dunes.

"Beautiful," she exhales.

"It doesn't compare to you," I observe, staring at her and meaning every word.

I want to build the bridge between us. Fix the upsets and stress of last night. She glances at me then returns her gaze to the rising sun.

"You say the dumbest things," she mutters in Common but a smile plays at the corners of her lips.

On impulse I put my arm around her shoulders. She doesn't move away or resist. We stand together, watching the suns rise and appreciating the beauty together.

I'm happy. Watching the suns crest the horizon I realize I'm content. This is the life I want, and it revolves around her.

11

AMARA

"This place sucks," I mutter.

Shidan says nothing. He's been quiet since this morning. I don't know if it's a good thing or not. It leaves a void and I hate to admit it but I miss his cheerfulness. I almost gave in last night. I wanted to, damn did I want to, but I can't. No one else is going risk themselves for me. It doesn't matter how big and sexy he is.

The heat beats down. I'm so hot that I quit sweating which isn't good. One more step, one more. Focus girl! One foot in front of the other. Damn sand slides when I put my foot down as we climb yet another stupid dune. This entire planet is nothing but dunes of god awful sand that gets into every thing. I've got sand in my boots, under my pants, hell I've got sand in my underwear. Shidan wants to help me, I should let him. No, that's stupid. He'd wear out then we'd be double screwed. No, I have to carry my weight. This was my bright idea in the first place. Ugh, should have sent Gershom's boys.

My head is pounding, another sign the heat's taking its toll. My vision doubles and when I put my foot down for my next step, the sand slides faster than I expect, throwing me forward. Raising my hands to catch myself I miss and slam against the ground, planting my face in the sand. The air rushes from my lungs as hit. I can't breathe, my lungs refuse to accept air back in. I'm pushing up, trying to rise, but the sand shifts and I can't do it.

Suddenly. I'm lifted into the air. Shidan has a grip on my backpack, using it like a handle to lift me out. I'm hanging two feet off the ground, dangling in his grip like a doll. Damn it he's strong! He doesn't appear to be straining in the slightest. It's effortless to lift me and my heavy pack.

"Put me down!" I gasp, desperately needed air rushing in as I kick my feet in mid-air.

He cocks his head to one side as a slow smile spreads across his face. "Of course, lyutik," he says, placing me on my feet.

"Didn't need your help," I mutter, dusting sand off.

"As you wish."

I glare at him but it doesn't phase him. I'm lying. I know it and he knows it too. I needed his help. Worse I still do. I can't do any of this on my own. I'm not strong enough. I'm not good enough. He crosses his arms over his chest, waiting for me to finish and I can't help but notice the way his biceps bulge. The early morning light sparkles on exposed scales making him look radiant. Why does he have to be so damned attractive?

"Quit looking at me like that," I grouse.

"As you wish, lyutik."

"Quit calling me that!"

Something about the way he says that pushes my buttons. Like I'm missing something. "I don't need your help!" I scream. "I can carry my own weight!"

My head pounds, my throat is dry and scratchy, and the

screaming isn't helping. Every muscle aches, deep down, like it's in my bones. I stop from exhaustion.

"When did you take epis?" Shidan asks, his voice soft, gentle, and much nicer than I deserve.

"Before we left."

He shakes his head then takes my pack from me. I'm too exhausted to resist and some part of me is grateful. I don't know how to show it to him though. What if I need him? Would that be so bad?

Yes. No one else will get hurt because of me.

Shidan digs through my pack and pulls out a leather-bound package which he opens. The few strands of epis lie exposed to the sun. Their color is fading, a sure sign they're losing potency. He offers a strand and I take it, grateful that he doesn't make a thing of it. Putting the strand into my mouth I close my eyes and savor the plant. The familiar sourness explodes on my tongue, followed by a spicy aftertaste. It's losing potency. I'm not a fan of spicy, fresh epis would make my eyes water. This isn't much stronger than some weak red pepper.

Still, it does the trick. I keep my eyes closed until the effects spread through my body. It works fast, bringing welcome relief. That's the best way to describe epis. When you're dying of thirst, which I am here on this hell hole piece of shit planet, epis is a cold drink of water. A sense of wellness spreads out from my stomach, a glowing ball of light that burns away all the bad things. The ache in my muscles fades as they relax and tension drains. My scratchy, dry throat soothes. Eyes that were burning and having trouble focusing cool and regain clarity. At last it reaches my head and the headache eases then fades away. Taking a deep breath, I sigh.

"Better?" Shidan asks.

"Yes, thanks."

Shidan nods then holds my pack up. I turn and slide my arms into the straps letting him help me put it back on. I can do that. It's okay. Doesn't mean I'm weak, he's being nice. Nothing wrong with being nice.

"There is an oasis a short distance away that Sverre told me about," he says. "If we can make it there, we can make camp and refill our water supply."

I want to argue with him but I can't. We've walked all night and into the day. I'm done. No matter how much I want to carry on, my body is reaching its limits.

"Fine," I say. "My epis supply won't hold out for long. It's already losing potency. We have to hurry, not to mention that Calista needs us."

"I know," he says, his mouth a grim, hard line.

There's nothing more to say about it so we walk. His idea of a short ways and mine must be different I come to realize after an hour more of walking. I haven't seen a sign of any oasis. Red damn sand broken by the occasional rock protrusion. This place sucks. Sucks so damn bad.

"How much further?" I ask.

"Not long now, lyutik," he says over his shoulder.

I roll my eyes. No matter how many times I ask him not to call me that he still does it. I don't know what it means. I've never heard the other Zmaj say it and it isn't in the embedded vocabulary in my head. It must not translate to Common. He's nice, too damn nice, and he always wants to help. It'd be so easy to let him but I know what happens then.

But his kiss! Damn he's a good kisser. The memory of his lips on mine, the pressure of his huge body pinning me to the wall comes back and I can't help but focus my attention on the way his erection dug into my stomach. It felt huge and if I didn't know better, I'd worry if we were compatible. We are, Calista and Jolie have proven that. Jolie has been coy about what Sverre is like down there but she's dropped hints.

Her and Calista both get the same far away look and knowing smile if the subject comes up. I know, without a shadow of a doubt, that sex with Shidan would be amazing.

The thing is, if I do that he'll want more. It wouldn't be just sex with him there'd be strings so thick I'd be in a web. I have to admit, if only to myself, the idea has an appeal. The way he looks at me, it'd be nice. If I was a different girl. If everything wasn't what it is.

Stop it. It's a damn merry-go-round in my head but I can't. That's it.

"There," Shidan says, pointing.

Climbing up the loose sand next to him I follow his finger and see a stand of trees in the distance. They have fat, bulbous bases that go straight up fifteen to twenty feet before branching out with thick limbs and foliage. Relief floods through me to see something besides more sand. Exhaustion lies heavy but seeing our goal, a second wind pushes it back.

"Okay." I give a wan smile.

"I can carry you," Shidan offers.

"Are you kidding me?"

He tilts his head to one side, staring at me then looks away.

Idiot, I should have said yes! Sure, I should have, if I was someone else. If I could open myself up. If, if, if, too many damn if's. Regret. Shidan is the kindest man I've ever known. Why can't I be nice to him?

"Let's go," I sigh.

I start down the dune and the sand slides from under my foot, then I'm on my ass and sliding down fast. I yelp as I scramble, trying to stop myself but the more I fight it the more the sand falls. I'm picking up speed until I'm flying down the dune. My foot catches on something hidden and I'm going fast enough it causes me to flip up into the air then I hit face first and continue my descent. Sliding to a stop, sand is in my mouth, my eyes, my ears, and through my hair. It's even more miserable than before.

As I try to climb to my feet Shidan is here helping. I take his hand and I'm grateful for it even if I don't want to be. My muscles quiver with adrenaline. I'm shaking uncontrollably. The good side is, my slide down the dune closed the distance with the oasis. But it hurts my pride, which is the worst part.

"Are you okay?" Shidan asks.

"I'm fine," I reply, dusting myself off.

I don't waste any more time. The distance isn't far and Shidan falls in next to me. The shade of the first trees stretches across the sand. I swear the temperature drops twenty degrees as I step into the shadows of the branches. I stop and sigh. Shidan stands close, quiet, waiting. Glancing up at him a slow smile spreads across my face.

"Made it this far," I say.

"Yes," he nods. "I will gather materials and make a shelter. We can rest for a while and refill our water."

"Okay," I say. "I will rest here by this tree."

He looks to where I point and nods then heads deeper into the oasis. He disappears behind the trunk of a tree before I drop my pack. Leaning against the strange tree I look around, taking in my surroundings. A beautiful, huge flower catches my eye. It has a large center that is reddish brown with long, floppy leaves that lay out around it. The entire thing has a rusty color set in a splash of green. It looks gorgeous so I go close to inspect it, being careful because I know everything on this planet is never as nice as it looks.

The leaves vibrate as I approach or maybe there's a slight breeze. I'm so hot and tired I can't be sure. I move as close as I can without stepping on any parts of it because I want to see the center portion. It's dark, almost black, which is odd. Wondering why, I lean in to get a good look when the hair on the back of my neck stands on end and fear runs down my spine. I jump back but I'm too late. The beautiful rust colored leaves snap shut on my head and grip tight. I pull back and scream at the same time but I can't get free.

I'm being pulled forward. Terrified, I scream again with everything I've got. A throat-tearing, primal sound that starts deep in my core and rips its way out of my throat. I swing my fists against the plant from the outside but to no avail. Struggling, my feet slip out from under me and I fall into the plant. It does some kind of weird push-pull, dragging me close to its center. Its grip is on my throat, making it hard to breathe. I gasp air each time the tension eases.

A loud thump. So loud it echoes through my ears and around my head. One thump follows another and another until it's a repeating pattern. The leaves gripping me shudder then spring apart and I fly backwards and away, landing on my ass. Shidan is wielding his staff-sword weapon they call a lochaber. He swings it around his head and circles in front of him and with each swing he slices into the plant. It waves its leaves and shudders trying to defend itself. Shidan is relentless in his assault until in moments the plant is nothing more than shredded foliage decorating the oasis.

"Are you okay?" he asks, dropping in front of me.

He takes my head in both his hands, tilting it to one side so he can inspect the wounds on my neck. He makes a tsking hiss sound then digs in his pack and pulls out a container.

"I'm fine," I say, pushing myself away.

"You're injured."

"I said I'm fine!" I say, angry at myself for having been so stupid. Nothing on this planet isn't trying to kill me. I know this. Why did I do that? How could I have been so damn stupid?

Shidan ignores my protests and slathers a smelly paste along my neck then, forcibly yet gently, pushes my head to the other side so he can tend the wounds there. He's close, and he smells musky, a man's man. I grab him and kiss him without thinking about it, pulling him close. He drops the salve and gives himself over to the kiss. His hands touch my legs pushing them apart, moving right to my pussy and rubbing it through my pants. He moans as he touches me. I'm wet. Desire is a roaring bonfire rising and out of control. I want him. I need him.

I can't have him. He'll only get hurt.

I break the kiss and push his hand away. He looks at me confused and I shake my head. There's no denying his erection, it's enormous. He leans in but I move back and shake my head again.

"No," I say. "I can't."

I'll hurt him. I'm no good for him. I can't be the woman he wants. I'm not a treasure to protect and I can't tease him along. He deserves someone better than me. His mouth opens like he's about to speak but then closes without saying a word.

Nodding, he stands up and sets up a shelter for us without a word.

I watch silently. Once he's finished, I lay down. The taste and feel of his lips against mine circles my mind as I drift to sleep.

12

SHIDAN

*a*mara lies on her side next to me. Holding my head up on my arm I watch her chest rise and fall as I study her curves. Committing them to memory. She's perfect. She stirs but I remain still, unwilling to wake her. I don't want this moment to end. This time with her where I can at least pretend she is mine. This time alone is what I need to show her how good our lives could be together. She is so strong. I think I'm understanding her. Maybe. She rolls onto her back and her eyes blink then open.

"Are you staring at me?" she asks.

"No," I say, my scales itch with the lie.

Amara rolls her eyes. "Yeah, right," she says, stretching her arms over her head.

The soft mounds of her chest compress as she stretches, the shirt pulls up revealing a hint of smooth, perfect, unscaled skin. I know how soft it is and my fingers tingle at the memory. My hand twitches as I resist my desire to touch her. She sits up, rolls her neck, then yawns. The suns are low in the sky and shadows are thickening through the oasis. I lean in closer, reaching to inspect her wounds.

"What are you doing?" she asks, scooting away.

"Your wounds lyutik."

"I'm fine," she says, standing up. "What do we have to eat?"

I dig through my pack and find guster meat. Amara stretches again then we sit down and eat.

"We should be to your ship before sunrise."

"Good," she says around a mouthful of meat.

We finish our meal then pack up our bags. I shoulder mine and hold out my hand, offering to take hers. Amara stares at my hand until I drop it. I shrug and smile as she shakes her head.

"I'll carry my own weight," she says, hefting her pack onto her shoulders.

As we turn to leave, I hear something. A whine, machine made, not natural. Its growing louder.

"Did you fill the water— " I put my hand on her mouth to silence her while straining my ears. "Hey! Don't yo— "

She cuts herself off now, hearing the sound I already heard. Her eyes widen and her mouth snaps shut.

"Hide!" I hiss and she nods.

The oasis doesn't have sand I can bury us in. Looking around, I point to two trees that aren't too far apart. Amara runs for one and ducks behind it. The whine becomes a deafening whir as the machine comes closer. I move towards the sound. I hear Amara's sharp intake of breath but I have to know what we are facing. Flattening myself against a different tree, I peek around to see the source.

Two Zzlo climb down off a land skimmer and walk into the shade of the oasis. They're both armed and dressed in their space leathers. They don't look around, making me certain they're not looking for us. The two men talk with each other in their harsh, guttural language. Something snaps behind me. I whirl around and see Amara with her mouth open and eyes wide. She's stepped out from behind the shelter of her hiding spot and was making her way towards me.

Damn it!

I glance back and see the two Zzlo's also heard it. They draw their weapons, coming closer.

Hide! I mouth at Amara motioning her back.

She drops low and crawls towards her hiding spot. I turn in towards the tree I'm hiding behind and climb up its bare trunk, finding small crevasses I can use as hand holds to pull myself higher. I'm above the eye level of the Zzlo by the time they pass underneath me. Watching them over my shoulder I count my dual heart beats to keep myself calm. One man is a few steps ahead of the other, weapon ready, closing with Amara's position.

I can't let them get to her. Pushing off with my legs as hard as I can, I spread my wings and I take to the air. The wind whistles, I flip, doing a backwards somersault in mid-air. As my feet come back to below me, I close my wings and drop like a rock, landing on top of the Zzlo furthest from Amara.

Burning laser shots whistle pass me as I crash into him. The other one is fast enough to have gotten off two shots before I land. The one I drop on collapses beneath me in a heap. I whirl towards the one still standing. He has his weapon aimed at me. I leap for him in the space of a breath.

A laser burns past my ear as he fires. I reach for his gun, my hand is almost there, then I'm stopped and falling. Something has my foot. I slam into the ground, hard, knocking the breath out of me. I gasp for air that won't come. Looking back, the other Zzlo I thought was out climbs to his feet. He has my ankle gripped in his hand and jerks, pulling me across the ground.

Flipping onto my back, I kick at him but he dodges. He

laughs, or it sounds like a laugh, but I have a surprise for him. I lash low with my tail taking his legs out. Curling into a ball, I throw my legs out and push off with my hands launching to my feet. I land in a crouch as the Zzlo rolls away.

He scrambles out of my reach then rolls over to his feet. We circle each other as I move so that he's between the other Zzlo and me. He makes more guttural sounds like grinding rocks. He feints in and I move back then he ducks low. The other Zzlo shoots at me but I'm ready for that, ducking low to keep his partner as a shield between us.

In a burst of speed I rush the Zzlo. I'm bigger than him and bring my weight to bear forcing him down. He brings a knee up into my gut causing me to loosen my grip and cry out in pain. I push past it bringing my fist up under his jaw. His teeth crack together when it hits and his head rocks back on his shoulders. He stumbles backwards but Amara yells jerking my attention to her.

The other Zzlo is aiming at me but hesitates when Amara yells. She hits that one over the head with a large stick. While I admire her bravery, he's wearing a helmet and the stick shatters against it without giving him pause. He whirls on her, swinging his fist which connects with the side of her head. Amara flies and crashes in a limp heap.

Fog encloses me as rage roars, consuming my thoughts. I give myself over to the bijass. Grabbing the Zzlo in front of me, his eyes widen in surprise as I hiss and lift him off his feet and over my head. He struggles and slips falling onto my head. He punches me, over and over, but I don't feel the pain. Amara lies on the ground a few feet away. Shaking her head, she crawls backwards, trying desperately to get away from the other Zzlo that is closing with her.

"RUN!" I scream.

I grab the Zzlo in my arms again. We struggle against each other until he breaks his way free. I push past him, knocking him behind me to go after the one threatening Amara. It's a mistake. He slams something into my back, throwing me forward. Pain pulses as the fog of bijass embraces me. It fuels the rage. I have to save her.

The Zzlo in front of me reaches for Amara as she scrambles. Time slows. The Zzlo's hand reaches for her one heartbeat at a time. I'm running through thick air. One step, another, I'm close. My fingers stretch for him, I must stop him, she is mine!

Something hits my back. A weight drags me down. Arms lock around my throat, pulling back, cutting off all air. Grabbing them, I try to break the hold but I can't get a grip. Blackness encroaches on my vision as the need for air grows. I give up trying to grip the arms and slam an elbow back into my assailant. He grunts and I strike again then again. His grip loosens and blessed air burns its way into my lungs.

The other Zzlo gets a grip on Amara and jerks her to her feet by her arm. She's limp, her head lolling side to side. The rage becomes all consuming. Muscles tremble as adrenaline pumps through me. They've hurt her. They will pay!

Arms clasp around me, pressing my wings tight and restraining my arms. I lean forward, pulling the Zzlo with me. He moves his feet to keep his balance and I bring my tail up between his legs, slamming it into his crotch. He screams in pain and shock. His armor absorbs some of the impact but not enough. His grip loosens, and he drops to the ground in a fetal position.

The one holding Amara jerks her in front of himself and pulls his gun, holding it to her head. We lock eyes. His dead, empty eyes are soulless. All he cares about is his own survival. He grunts, motioning with his head but the gun never wavers. Amara moans then her eyelids flutter. My heart leaps even as my blood boils. She's coming around.

"Wha— " Amara starts, then the Zzlo pulls his arm around her neck tighter, pressing the gun closer.

Her eyes widen and her mouth forms an O. She looks at me but I keep my focus on him. One mistake. Any opening. I'll find it. I will save her.

One moment stretches into another. Our standoff continues. My tail shifts back and forth, my wings rustle, I force my balled hands to relax. Rising from my crouch I hold my hands out in front of myself, palms up. He looks from my hands to my eyes then back at my hands. The gun moves away from her head. An inch, no more, but it's enough. I leap.

He reacts, pulling the gun from her and aiming at me. Its instinct and what I wanted him to do. The gun fires and blazing electricity cuts through the air. I turn my shoulder into it and take the shot. My left arm goes numb and falls useless to my side. Amara, alert, beautiful and brilliant, spins, tripping and falling free of his loosened grip.

I hit him, my right shoulder connects with his neck, snapping his head back. Rage. All consuming. He hurt her. His fists pound my head forcing me backwards. My left side is useless, feeling nothing. I swing and he ducks.

"Shidan!" Amara screams.

A knife appears in his hand. He moves away from Amara as the two of us circle each other. He slashes the air with the knife, a long blade with a wicked, jagged side. A slow grin spreads across the pirate's face. My hearts beat faster as rage rises higher. Red tinges my vision and it narrows until there is only him. He slashes a feint forward and I move, stepping to the side. Turning, I slam into him with my numb left side.

He tries to bring his knife back between us but I'm too quick. He's thrown off balance, stumbling. Pressing the attack, I grab his arm and pull back. He tries to plant his feet but I heave, jerking him closer. Just beyond I see Amara. Her face swells from bruising, tears are in her eyes, and her torn shirt reveals a patch of delicate, soft skin.

The Zzlo swings at me with his free arm. I duck under it, jerking down on the arm in my grip. There's a loud pop as his shoulder dislocates and he cries out in pain. He convulses and the knife in his other hand drops. I lose my grip and he slips out, diving for the gun. I can't stop him so I dive for the knife.

Rolling, I grab the weapon, landing in a crouch. The Zzlo is running for the gun. I leap, spreading my wings. I'm off balance. My left side is tingling with numbness. Raising the knife I fly and slam into him as I land, driving the knife home. He grunts, then goes limp as it plunges through his space armor. Rage consumes me and I stab him over and over. Rising, covered in gore, I spin around. The other Zzlo lies limp with his head at an odd angle.

Amara rises to her feet, looking at me with a mix of fear and admiration. Dropping the knife I close the gap between us and take her in my arms, lifting her off her feet. Our lips meet with bruising force. My prime penis pounds with need as it presses hard against her middle. Instinct, primal need, blended by rage and the bijass.

She doesn't resist. Her body melds to mine. She is mine. No one can hurt her.

13

AMARA

*N*o one has ever stood up for me like that. If it wasn't for him I'd be dead or worse. Shidan takes me into his arms and I plant my lips onto his. My skin tingles, butterflies in my stomach, and everywhere he touches me a fire burns.

Wrapping my arms around his neck we spin a slow circle as he holds me up off my feet. My heart pounds in my chest. As the fear and adrenaline subside, my mind clears and I pull back from the kiss. Our eyes lock for an instant then he pushes in for another. I pull back but he doesn't stop. I try to hold him back with my arms but he pushes past them and takes the kiss. His lips against mine.

"No," I say, breaking the kiss again and pushing against his shoulders.

He doesn't listen. He kisses me again despite my efforts to stop. Squirming in his arms I set my feet back on the ground and brace them. When I break the kiss this time I push, hard. He stumbles back, eyes widening, then his foot catches on a limb. He falls backwards with his arms pinwheeling. I reach for him but too late. He falls into the water of the oasis with a loud splash. He rises, spluttering, and I can't hold back my laughter. Anger flashes in his eyes and across his face then he looks down and shakes his head. When he looks up again, his eyes are clear.

"I'm sorry lyutik," he says, but I'm still laughing.

"You're all wet."

He looks down and shrugs then he does the unexpected. He peels off his clothes. As he moves, his muscles ripple. The water runs across his scales catching sunlight and setting off a rainbow of sparkles. Desire hits like a rushing tide, pulling me under. My mouth turns dry under the raging assault of the fire in my core that roars to life.

Shidan doesn't stop and I can't look away. The way his muscles ripple, the gleam of his scales, the burning desire in his eyes. His hands undo the fasten of his pants and they fall away. He wraps them into a ball tosses the wet cloth which lands with a splosh at my feet

His cock is enormous and erect. It's different, exotic. Ridges run along the top, smooth raised mounds that march down to his pelvis where the largest ridge at the base of his cock protrudes. The ridges make me wonder how it would ever fit inside without causing damage. I know it works, I'm not the first human female that's mated with a Zmaj, but damn. And the size of it!

It looks like it's as bigger around than my fist and almost as long as my forearm. I've never seen anything like it. The guys in my squad always thought it was fun to expose themselves when I was around to try to shock me. It was a game they played because I was the only girl but even the largest among them didn't compare to Shidan.

The water runs across his scaled chest and drips off his erection. Tearing my eyes from his cock, I look up. Something passes between us and I know he wants me. And I want him, want to feel his cock sliding in and filling me. I want to know what those ridges feel like, pressing into my body.

Wetness forms between my legs thinking about it. Ignoring all the reasons not to, I walk into the water. He smiles as I come closer then reaches out. Rising onto my toes our lips meet as his arms engulf me. I moan into the kiss. His cock digs into my stomach, crushed between us.

His tongue pierces my lips, forcing its way in.

Doubt rises in my mind. I shouldn't do this. I don't want him to get hurt.

He grabs my ass and squeezes, pulling my cheeks apart. Fingers graze between my legs and I shiver, squashing any further doubts.

Hands roam around my ass and up my back. Reaching down, I grab my shirt and pull it over my head, leaning back. His eyes go to my tits and widen in surprise. An instance of self-consciousness hits me.

"Amazing," he says, his voice filled with awe.

A flush races across my skin. I toss the shirt towards land and he pulls me up higher. Wrapping my legs around his waist I thrust my chest forward. His mouth is hot and his tongue flicks my nipple. He holds me up with one arm around my waist the other hand plays with my free nipple. Electric jolts pulse from the hard point in his mouth pounding into my core. Nothing has ever felt better.

Closing my eyes I lean my head back. He carries us deeper into the water while his mouth moves on my breast. He circles my nipples, sucks, and then pulls back. A moan escapes my lips. He's amazing. The warm water touches my legs as he walks us in until it's up to my ass.

I want him inside. My clitoris throbs with need. Running my hands along his face while he continues to lick my tits I grind against him. I need more.

"Shidan," I gasp.

He looks up, desire burning in his eyes. I reach a hand underneath myself and stroke along his cock. It jumps under my touch and the fire in his eyes burns hotter. He lowers me to my feet. The warm water climbs my legs as he sets me down. As it touches my pussy it feels so good I almost orgasm.

He takes my head between his hands and I lean back into his kiss. Our tongues dance together while I squirm out of my pants. The water makes it difficult but I manage and toss them to land with my shirt. Shidan's hand passes down across my breasts and cups my pussy. He massages the lips without penetrating and once more I'm moaning into his kiss. He teases my body like an expert. My desire builds until every nerve is on fire.

Grabbing his cock I stroke it up and down focusing my attention on the underside. The top ridges are hard but the underside is the silkiest thing I've ever felt. He groans and his hips thrust back and forth. His finger pushes inside my pussy and I shudder.

He hooks his finger, and it grazes my clit with each push in and out. An orgasm builds as my core winds tighter. I don't know how much more of this I can stand. I've needed nothing more in my life, I want his cock.

I jump up and wrap my legs around him, splashing water. Shidan catches me and his hands hook under my legs to hold me without breaking our kiss. I lower myself down until I feel the head of his cock at my opening. I push down until the first ridge causes resistance. Just the head of his cock feels amazing, but it's not enough.

We're surrounded by warm, lubricating water. It helps as he pushes deeper, his kiss gentle but insistent. I pant as I slide lower, taking him further inside. The first ridge enters. It drags across my clitoris and I tremble with pleasure.

Weakness and desire assault me until in one sudden

motion I slide down onto his cock taking him all the way in. The hard ridge on his pelvis push past my protective folds and the largest ridge at the base of his penis crushes into my clit. The pleasure is like a bomb. He thrusts up once and I lose myself, my orgasm wracks my body and I clench my legs tighter around Shidan.

I feel his cock pulse inside, filling me, he's just as incapable of holding back as I am. I'm left breathless in his arms. His cock softens so I pull myself up by wrapping my arms around his neck to steady myself. It leaves an emptiness behind as his cock leaves my pussy but it's a satisfying emptiness. As I let myself back down I'm surprised to feel his erection is back in full. I open my eyes to see his smiling face.

"Seriously?" I ask, laughing.

"That was only one," he says, like that explains everything.

"One?"

"Of my cocks."

"How many do you have?" I ask in shock.

"Two, do human men not?"

I shake my head, unable to form words but my body is already responding to him. You'd think Calista or Jolie would have mentioned two cocks! He pistons in and I clench my fists in his hair, gasping. This time we go slower. Connecting and letting the sensations and pleasure build.

His cock slides in, easier this time, my body has adjusted to his unusual anatomy. The ridges increase my pleasure. Each time they pass it pulls on my clitoris, brushing it, heightening the sensations of sex. My breath comes in gasps that match Shidan's as we press our foreheads together. We share breath as his large hands cup my ass, lifting and thrusting me on his cock.

Would it be so bad to have someone who cares about me? I want to let him in, to give myself to him but some part of me still holds back. I care for him. I can't deny it even to myself anymore, but can I let him be my protector?

For now, in this moment, I forget all that. A small part of me remains locked away.

Shidan nips my lower lip with his teeth, pulling all my attention back to the moment. He grunts and clenches my ass, slamming me harder and faster. The base ridge grinds my clit and a stronger orgasm than I've ever felt locks my body. I mewl into his mouth as I lock my arms around his head, panting into his neck as every muscle I have spasms. I slowly grind as the last moments of pleasure clenching deep inside milk Shidan's orgasm from his cock. He screams my name as he comes. Satisfaction fills me as we kiss then extricate ourselves from each other.

Those pirates might not have been alone and we still have to get to the wrecked ship.

14

SHIDAN

a strange feeling swells in my stomach and out through my limbs. My tail twitches, my wings flutter, it's as if there's an itch I can't scratch. Watching Amara wring the water from her clothes before putting them on makes me feel this way. She is mine and I am hers. Joining with her was even better than I imagined. The connection between us is strong, alive, and vibrant.

I splash warm water up and across my chest and face then climb out. It pleases me when I notice her glancing at my cock. A smile plays around the corner of her lips then she shakes her head. I've known since the moment I saw her outside the dome she's meant to be mine. It was a certainty that filled me and hasn't left since. It took time but none of that matters. She's more than worth the wait.

I've never met a stronger woman. My face is becoming sore because I can't stop my smile. It's stretching the muscles beyond anything I've experienced before. I pull my clothes on but I can't take my eyes off of her. The wet clothes cling to her body accenting her curves and the soft mounds of her breasts. So strange, her breasts. Strange, exotic and erotic.

Her hard nipples poke through the shirt, outlined by damp-ness. My mouth waters with the desire to roll my tongue around them. My prime penis stiffens again. Amara glances over, sees where my gaze is, then the tenting of my pants.

"Uh-uh," she says, shaking her head. "We've got a job to do, remember?"

"Of course, lyutik."

We gather our supplies and walk. The suns are low in the sky and it will be dark soon. Traveling at night seems to have been a good idea. I would never have thought so but we've not run into any of the night hunters, so far at least.

"How much farther do you think?" Amara asks after a short while.

"Not long," I say, shielding my eyes and staring ahead.

"Good," she says, exhaling.

"Are you okay?"

"Yeah."

She's lying. I know she's lying because I can feel it. It's a heaviness between us that wasn't there before but I don't know what's wrong. She shifts her pack on her shoulders then walks.

"I can carry that," I offer, holding out a hand.

She looks at me over her shoulder, her mouth becoming a hard line. My hand drops to my side. I guess things haven't changed that much. She shakes her head and resumes walk-ing. I hurry to catch up.

"Damn it's hot," she mutters.

"You should take more epis."

She nods, letting the pack slide from her shoulders. We kneel together while she digs through and finds the plant. She opens the oiled leather in her hand to reveal one strand of epis. It's no longer blue and has no glow, a dull brown meaning it's lost most of its value.

A sick feeling hits me in my stomach. We're days from

being able to return to the city. I expected the epis to last longer. Out here in the suns she needs to take epis more than she does under the protective dome. Her body has no built up stores and is still being changed by the plant to handle the heat.

She stares and shakes her head. "Crap," she exhales.

I don't speak. I can't. Fear slides in behind the sick feeling. This is dangerous. Too dangerous. She can't stay out here. I have to get her back to the city, back to a fresh supply of epis. I don't know how long she can go without it. She takes the strand and places it in her mouth, chews, then chases it down with some water.

"We need to go back," I say.

Her eyes harden. "No," she says. "We can't. Calista and Jolie need this. They're counting on us, there's no option, no choice. We have to succeed."

Her strength and determinism shine through and my love for her explodes in response. My admiration, my love, my need for her are overwhelming. Words won't come out so I nod. She closes her eyes and inhales deeply. She closes the pack up then stands and puts it back on her shoulders.

"We should hurry," she says.

"Let me carry the pack," I offer again.

She looks at me defiantly then something crosses her face and grimacing, she nods. She hands me the pack and we start off.

"This place is hell," she mutters in her own language.

"What is hell?" I ask in Common.

She stops and turns, her eyes wide. Her mouth opens then closes, and she shakes her head. "What did you say?"

I smile, feeling awkward and try to defuse her anger. "What is hell?"

"Are you kidding me?" she says, shaking her head again. "No, no, no."

"I do not understand."

"You…" she trails off staring. "When? How? Do all of you?"

"Aren't you happy?" I ask in confusion. I thought she would be. I learned her language to honor her. To show her how much I care. She seems angry and I don't understand.

"Like?" she explodes, her hands fly up into the air and she shakes her head in disbelief. "You've been lying! Why would I like that? How long?"

"I do not understand, what do you mean?"

"I mean how long have you been able to understand what we say? Do all of you know our language? Is this some big inside secret you and your Zmaj buddies have been having a big laugh about?"

"No."

"No what? No you're not laughing about it or no it's not a secret? No what?"

This is not going the way I expected. I hold up my hands hoping to calm her down but her beautiful face flushes red.

"Lyutik," I say, reverting to my language.

"Don't call me that!"

"Amara," I say instead. "Please, I do not understand." This is wrong. How did it go so wrong?

"How long?" her voice is low, a growling sound.

"I'm not sure," I answer. "A while now."

"Why didn't you tell me?"

"I wanted to… surprise you," I shrug.

"Surprise me," she mutters, turning her back and staring off across the desert. "I thought we were getting somewhere. I trusted you."

A knife stabs into my hearts. I take a step back because the pain in my chest is hard and sharp. "Amara…" I trail off, my mouth and throat dry.

"Let's go," she says, taking her pack from me, hitching it up and walking away.

"Amara!"

"What?" She whirls on one foot.

"Please— "

"Please what?" she cuts me off. Amara shakes her head, grits her teeth, then turns and marches.

"Amara, please," I say again, but she doesn't stop.

I run after her and grab her shoulder, turning her to face me. Tears well in her eyes.

"I trusted you," she chokes out at last.

Shaking my head, I try to knock loose words, any words that will fix this. I thought it would make her happy. My intentions were pure, good, but now it's all wrong.

"Amara, no, I wanted to show you," I say.

"Show me? What? That you were spying on me? How long Shidan? How long have you been able to speak Common? How many of my conversations have you listened in on?"

"Not long, I…" I trail off, thinking of the things I've heard her say.

She shakes her head, water streaming down her cheeks. "You must think I'm horrible."

"No!" I exclaim, surprised at the change in direction.

"How can you not? I've said so many mean things about you and now you've heard them all! Space and stars why am I such a bitch?"

Tears flow and she wipes at them. Her body shakes as she sobs and I feel her pain even if I don't understand it. I reach out, placing my arms around her. I pull her closer but she stiffens then jerks herself free. She inhales then wipes the tears and turns her back.

"We need to go, now," she says, her voice resolute.

"Okay," I say, stepping up beside her but she steps one step to the side and walks.

When Amara stops walking, I go two steps beyond her before I realize it and stop too. I turn to look at her and she points. Following her finger I realize we've arrived.

AMARA

*J*ust get this over with and get back, I think looking at the wreck of what was once my home.

A wave of nostalgia rises. Home. Life was both easier and harder on the ship. Easier in that nothing was trying to kill me which is a regular occurrence on this hell-hole of a planet. Harder because every day was another challenge to prove myself worthy. No matter how long I was a member of the fighter squadron, they never accepted me. Every day I had to prove myself over again.

Still, I miss it.

I miss the other pilots, the challenge, I miss flying. Damn do I miss flying.

What I don't miss is other people getting hurt because of my actions. A cycle I seem to be racing headlong into again.

My head is pounding, my mouth is as dry as the sand we're walking across, and standing here is doing nothing to make any of it better. Shidan moves closer, again, and again I take a step away. I can't believe he speaks Common. How much did he hear? How many mean things have I said he understood?

The worst part is I didn't mean most of them. There's no excuse for what I've done though. He deserves better. Better than I can be.

"Come on, let's get moving," I say, marching ahead.

The wreck is massive. The closer we get, the more of the sky it blots out. Shielding my eyes, I look up at it and smile. Memories of flying around the ship on maneuvers fill my thoughts. Then I was free. Nothing could stop me.

"It is most impressive," Shidan says.

"Yeah," I agree.

"Do you miss it?"

"Yes," I answer without thinking.

I see him nodding out of the corner of my eye. He walks over and places a hand on the cold steel of the generation ship. My home. Where I should be now, living my life so that my great-grandchildren could start theirs on their new home. A home I would never have seen. I'm not supposed to be here.

Shidan stares, pulling me out of the miasma of my thoughts.

"What?" I ask.

He smiles and shakes his head. "We should hurry," he says, turning away.

"Shidan you're a terrible liar."

"It is nothing," he says over his shoulder.

I bite my tongue before I call him out. He's right, we should hurry. We need to get back. The pounding in my head makes that clear. The epis effect is fading fast and I need to get more soon. I don't have time to figure out what he's thinking.

"This way," I say, pushing past him and leading the way.

The suns are behind the ship, casting a long shadow. It's a

relief to not be in the direct heat. My headache recedes. A hot, dry wind shifts the sand and the sound of a flapping tarp tells me we're close to the open side of the wreck. Before Calista and Ladon led us to his city, Rosalind had teams working to make the wreckage livable.

Sand has piled up in front of the shredded tarp. Shidan puts a hand on my shoulder then steps in front of me, drawing his staff blade and holding it ready.

"What are— "

He puts a finger to my mouth, shaking his head. Shrugging, I let him take the lead. What am I going to do, push him aside? He's right anyway. Who knows what could have taken up residence inside. Shidan slides the tarp to one side with the tip of his blade and stares into the shadows. He waits for several heartbeats before pressing in. I follow and we both stop just inside, letting our eyes adjust to the dimness. The place doesn't look much different from when we left. Shidan pushes me down to a crouch with a hand on my shoulder. He stares at me then explores the immediate area while I wait.

"It seems clear," he says.

"Good," I say. "Let's find what we need."

"What does it look like?"

"No clue."

"That's not helpful."

"Tell me about it," I say. "We need to go this way though. The medical bay will be up there."

I point up the inclined deck. This section of the ship landed on its tip so what was the floor and ceiling are now the walls. It's sitting at an angle buried into the sand so it's climbable but it won't be easy. My first concern is figuring out if there's power and whether we're being bombarded by lethal doses of radiation.

"How far up?" he asks.

"It's on the deck above us."

"Deck?" he asks. He doesn't know about ships, how could he?

"I'll show you," I say. "First things first, we need to figure out if there's power to the doors."

Stacked crates of supplies remain where we left them. Grabbing some, I create a stairway up to a door. Shidan observes for a moment then helps. It doesn't take long before we have a serviceable contraption. It may not be elegant but it's functional which is all I care about. I lead the way up and, standing on my tiptoes, I can just reach the keypad of the door.

My breath trembles as I touch the pad. Something so simple, which was a part of my daily life, a door pad. Its cool, hard plastic is a touch of the familiar. Please, please light up. I stroke my fingers across the screen and the familiar blue glow appears.

"Yes!" I exclaim.

"Good?" Shidan asks from right below me.

"Yes, there's power."

"Good."

I punch in my access code and the door shudders then slides part-way open before it jams.

"Damn it," I growl. "It's stuck. Push me up."

"What?"

"Push me up, I can't reach the opening."

Shidan's strong grip grabs my thighs and lifts me like I weigh nothing. No matter how many times he displays it, I'm always taken back by his strength. Impressive doesn't cover it. I grab onto the bottom section of the door. Straining, I pull myself up and over to the other side where I fall through the door and slam against the wall that is now the floor thanks to the angle of the ship.

"Ouch!" I exclaim as I slam down.

"Amara, are you okay?" Shidan calls. His head pops through the door and looks around till he spots me.

"Yeah, I'm fine," I say, climbing to my feet and rubbing my bruised backside.

Shidan shimmies through the opening, having a much harder time than I did getting through because of his much greater bulk. His wings and tail hang up as he tries to squeeze his body past. He works his way into the room and then drops with more grace than I did, landing on his feet.

"What is this place?" he asks, looking around.

"Waiting room."

We're in a small room with chairs bolted to the floor because it's a space ship and my ancestors designed things with that in mind. When we lived here though, I never thought about it. The other girls have talked about how they could go through their entire lives without thinking about the fact they lived on a spaceship. I saw it all the time as a fighter pilot but I loved it.

"Where do we need to go?"

"There," I tell him, pointing to a door on the opposite side of the room about halfway up the wall opposite the door we fell through.

Shidan nods then looks around. This room doesn't have the debris that the other side had, leaving nothing to stack into a ladder. Reaching up, Shidan tests one chair and finds it's bolted well enough he doesn't spend a lot of energy trying to get it free.

"I'll lift you up," he says.

"Can you get me high enough?"

He shrugs instead of answering as he moves to stand below the doorway. Closing my eyes, I take a deep breath then let it out. I don't know if I'm hoping for a bright idea or finding my resolve. I'm not sure I find either but when I open my eyes, I push forward.

Shidan bends at his knees, grips me by my waist and lifts me over his head. I still have to stretch my arm out to touch the keypad. It lights up and I punch in my code holding my breath while I do. My code is military clearance but I'm not sure it will let me into this area. When I hear gears engage and the doors slide, I breathe a sigh of relief. This set doesn't stick, opening all the way. I grip the edge and as I pull myself up Shidan shifts his grip down my legs to my feet.

Swinging through the opening I sit and look in before I drop. This room was an actual medical area. Attached to the floor-slash-wall are beds with heavy machines at the ends. Along what is now the floor below me are piles of carts, supplies, and miscellaneous machines. What I'm looking for should be down there.

I've seen the portable scanners medics carried with them. They'd bring them to our barracks for fast checkups or if there was an emergency. One of those should be perfect for finding out what's happening inside Calista. It will scan her then put out a three dimensional projection along with a medical analysis of what it found to be abnormal. Including the fact she has an alien baby growing inside her.

"Are you okay?" Shidan asks.

"Yeah," I say. "Just musing."

"Oh."

His hands grip the open door beside me and then he hauls himself up. I scoot over, making room for him as he struggles to shift himself around to sit as I am. He looks the room over in a long moment of silence.

"Why are there so many beds here? Is this a sleeping quarter?"

"No, this is medical."

"Oh. Is all this… necessary?"

I never thought about it. There are dozens of beds ready for patients. As the military clinic, this area was prepared for disaster or an attack from, well, nasty space pirates. Wounded would be brought here for treatment.

"I don't know," I sigh, turning to dig through the piles on the floor.

"What is it we need?" he asks.

"A big bag, orange, about like this." I hold my hands about three feet apart and then two feet wide.

We look for a long time. There's so much stuff piled up that it takes forever to search. There's not enough room to organize, so it's a matter of piling crap from one place to another. I don't know how long we've been at it but my stomach grumbles and my headache is growing worse. Shidan lifts a box and there behind it is the bag I'm looking for, at last!

"There!" I point, and Shidan tosses the box in his hands aside.

I check out the bag he found. Unzipping it reveals the machine. Two switches, one marked on, so I flip that one and it hums to life.

"It works?" Shidan asks.

"Yes!" I exclaim. "This is what I wa— "

I'm cut off by a loud bang outside the room. Shidan and I look at each other than move back over to the still open door. Sounds of booted footsteps ringing on metal comes through followed by guttural grunts.

I know those voices. Pirates. They found us.

The look on Shidan's face is clear, he wants to fight them but that's not smart. We don't know how many of them there are and we're not well armed.

Shidan reaches up for the door but stops as I place my hand on the bulging muscles of his arm. When he looks down at me, his eyes are soft and my heart skips a beat. No matter how mean I've been to him, and now I know he's understood me, he always looks at me like this. He treasures me. My good and my bad, he takes it all and still wants me. Maybe I've been a fool. Right now though, I need to focus on survival.

I place my finger over my lips. First, I have him help me close the med bay door and then I make my way across the room to the far side. There's another door here which I gesture towards. Shidan picks up on my hand signals and lifts me so I can open it. Once that's done, he lifts me through and follows. On the far side of this door I have him lift me again and close it.

"We can talk now," I whisper. "The doors should keep them from hearing us."

"We need to know how many there are."

"I know, I have an idea."

This was the observation chamber so there are computers built into the walls. Those walls now being the floor much like the rest of the ship, I crouch down and work the screens. The first four I try don't work but the last one glows to life. Shidan hovers as I work and I have to wonder how this must look to him. This is my home, my civilization, but to him it has to be foreign and exotic.

The computers are running, slow, but operating. I'm not a computer nerd but I get into the security cameras of the ship and then we have a view of what's going on in the main hallways. It's pirates like we thought. As the screen flickers and comes into focus, Shidan hisses. A dozen of them are tramping around out there and those are just the ones we can see. The worst part is, they look like they're planning to stay for a while.

We're screwed. One hundred percent screwed. I flip through camera views and the situation only gets worse. They have some kind of large vehicle parked outside that they're loading down with equipment and supplies. The bastards are scavenging the remains of my ship! It doesn't take a leap to realize they'll stay until they've filled their transport. I look over my shoulder at Shidan.

"There's a lot of them," he says.

"Yeah," I say. "We need to hide. Wait them out."

"Where?"

"Here. I can activate security on the door, should keep them out."

Shidan nods, stills staring at the monitor.

"What will we do while we wait?" I ask.

"Oh, I can think of a couple of things," he smiles.

SHIDAN

*H*er soft lips against mine push away all concerns. I'm forgiven, and that's all that matters. She's taking me back into her arms. I trail my lips across hers then her tongue darts out and licks mine as I pull back. I can't stop my smile. Her arms around my neck pulling me down are delicate, soft, and so welcome. Trailing the tips of my fingers up and down her spine she shudders, pressing herself against me and my body reacts as her breasts crush against my chest. My cock hardens into its fullness.

I want to consume her. Pull her into me until we are one.

She welcomes me, her mouth opening, my tongue drives in seeking and finding hers. As our tongues meet, the metaphor of us completes. Our bodies meld together, a pale shadow of our souls entwining. She is my treasure; I want her more than anything, nothing in the universe can compare to her, the way she makes me feel. My need for her is all-consuming.

I trail my lips along her neck, following the line to her shoulder then lower myself before her so I can trail kisses between her amazing breasts. She grabs her shirt and rips it over her head, throwing it aside. As she frees her breasts, her nipples harden in the cool air. Cupping them in my hands I kiss around her stomach while protecting them from the air.

She's delicate yet so strong. Her strength amazes me. She hooks her hands behind my head pressing me tight against her as I kiss my way around her stomach. The sweet taste of her is enough to drive me mad. My cock is throbbing, ready to explode, but I push it aside. We have time and I want to enjoy every inch of her.

"Shidan," she moans as my tongue trails up towards her breasts.

Her hips thrust against me while she pulls on my head, bringing me somehow closer still. Kneading her breasts while my tongue laps at her skin seems to heighten her pleasure. She groans then her hips gyrate against me. I want to take her so bad it's blinding. It takes an effort of will to keep control.

She undoes her pants and slides them off while I'm busy teasing the underside of her breasts with my tongue. She stumbles backwards as she works her legs free of the pants. I slide across the floor helping keep her on her feet until her back is against the wall. Kissing my way down I drag my tongue, tasting her, loving her.

My hearts pound in my chest. We feel so close, as one, she is open. She's holding nothing back and I'm so happy to be with her. Nothing in the world matters more. Feelings well up in my core until I'm sure they will explode. I look up and her soft eyes meet mine and she's there. We meet on a level I've never experienced, in a way I didn't know existed. I fall into her eyes as we become one.

Dragging my tongue across her hip I kiss her leg down to the knee then work my way up with soft kisses and nibbles. She shivers, goosebumps racing across her skin as I work my way towards her core. Her hands run through my hair then grip my shoulders as I approach her middle.

Tasting her is heaven. My tongue delights in the flavor of her as I part her sweet, soft folds. I work slowly, moving on instinct, inexperienced and uncertain in what I'm doing but feeling my way. I listen to her soft sounds, feel the way her body responds, using my senses as a guide.

She's wet and grows wetter as I work my tongue deeper. She moans and then her grip on my shoulders tightens and she thrusts her hips forward. Gripping her hips with my hands I help support her as I continue exploring with my tongue. As I work my way to the top of her opening, she's panting. Opening her folds with my tongue I find a hard nub. Circling it she goes wild, thrusting forward, gasping my name.

A treasure, like her. I circle this new delight and her wetness increases. I drag my tongue around then flick across the hard nub and she cries out. Her hands move to behind my head and she pulls me in tight. I let her pull me forward, guiding me towards her pleasure. It forces my tongue to flatten out across the hard nub. Moving my head side-to-side makes her breath come even faster, in shorter gasps.

I change directions, moving up and down then alternate side to side. Her breathing becomes faster until there's no pause between gasps. Her body stiffens, her hips thrust forward, and her grip on my head tightens holding me close. I don't move. Her legs quiver, her stomach against my fore-head vibrates as her pleasure takes her over the edge. She arches her back and makes a wordless sound then she shudders and her muscles shake with weakness. Her legs give out but I hold her until it passes.

"Shidan." She exhales my name, and it's the most beautiful sound I've ever heard.

Looking up at her from my knees, she is everything, my

universe is complete because she is it. She lowers herself until our eyes are level then she leans in and we kiss. Her tongue pierces my lips, she kisses me aggressively, passionate and sure of herself. Her hand grabs my cock through my pants then works its way inside the cloth.

When she touches my cock, I almost explode. Her softness against my hardness is almost too much to bear. I groan and she chuckles into our kiss as her hand grips then strokes.

"Want me?" she teases.

"Always."

"I'm yours," she says.

Looking into her eyes I see myself reflected. She kisses me and as our lips touch, impossibly I expand and grow.

Her love is my strength. We kiss and kiss and together we become stronger than ourselves. We become more in our unity than two. I lay her back without breaking our kiss. Her legs wrap around my hips, holding me close.

My throbbing cock is at her opening. As the tip slides in she groans and I sigh into our kiss. Sweet relief at the first touch of her to my member. I slide into her easily, her body taking me with slick greed, to the first ridge of my cock. Stopping there as I first meet resistance I hold myself over her.

We kiss, soft, gentle kisses breaking between each for breath. She wiggles her hips pushing for me to enter her the rest of the way. I push forward letting her body adjust to my girth. My cock breaks through and her body closing around me is overwhelming. My vision turns black to a field of stars. She is here, with me, in the stars. She is light and purity, love and strength. I give myself into her and she takes me as our bodies join into one.

Each thrust of my body becomes a joining. Loving her transports me to this new realm as the sensations continue to build until I'm dancing on the edge with her in my arms.

My core tightens and I'm close. She cries out in pleasure and I fall over the edge. We fall together into the brightness of each other.

My cock spasms again and again as it pumps my load into her and I collapse. We lie in each other's arms, kissing. Somehow this time was even more special. My love for her is boundless and only grows.

"That was amazing," she exhales, catching her breath at last.

"Yes."

She shifts closer resting her head on my shoulder. We lie together staring up.

"Well," she says at last. "It looks like we' re stuck here for a while."

"So it would seem."

"Whatever will we do to pass the time?" she asks, turning towards me with her full lips pouting.

"Oh I might have an idea," I say as I kiss her lips and my second cock rises to the occasion.

17

AMARA

I feel weak. Days have passed while we hide and watch the pirates scavenge the ship. My body needs epis, badly. Now I'm not only feeling the effects of dehydration but also of withdrawal from the plant. I couldn't even have sex with Shidan last night, which has been our only way to pass the time. I didn't know two people could have that much freaking sex.

A fever started early this morning and now I'm dizzy on top of the pounding headache, nausea, and overall sluggish feelings. This sucks. Shidan has been rationing our food supply and I know he's eating less than he needs to help me. I don't have the energy to argue with him about it. The only time I feel any better is right after eating some of the guster meat. He says they eat epis, infusing their meat with traces of it, which is why it helps.

My vision shimmers when I try to focus. Shidan's only a few feet away, watching the pirates on the monitor but it's hard to see. He's worried and not bothering to hide it. Hell, I'm worried too. We need to get back to the city and not just for Calista. I'm not sure how long it will be before my body gives up.

Reaching for my water bottle I almost have it when my fingers spasm and it falls over with a clatter. Shidan moves fast, too fast for me to follow, and he's here holding the bottle. The cool, refreshing liquid passes my parched lips and soothes my throat. I drink, grateful for the relief, even if it's only momentary.

"You're getting worse," he observes.

"I'm fine," I answer, pushing the bottle away.

Even the water is in limited supply. Shidan stares, frowning, then shakes his head as he moves back to the monitor. Leaning my head back, I close my eyes and let my thoughts drift. The fever is making it hard to keep track of time. I shiver even though the heat is sweltering. I don't want Shidan to know I'm seeing things. Impossible things from my past. Memories mixing with the present.

"Lean back," the medic orders and I comply. "What happened?"

"Slipped in the shower sir," I answer.

A giggle comes from the bed next to the one I'm sitting on. Draker is there, watching to see if I tell the truth. If Command finds out the other men did this, they'll come down hard. I already don't fit in and that would make sure I never will. I'll be the weak one forever. The snitch who can't handle my business.

"Uh-huh," the medic says. "Strangest shower wounds I've ever seen."

"Yes sir," I say, noncommittal.

"All right, well keep this ointment on it," he says, handing me a tube of cream. "Should heal in a few days. And be careful in the... shower."

"Yes sir," I say, jumping off the table.

Draker falls in behind me as I exit the med bay. "All better Stancher?"

"I'm fine."

"*Good. You know you're not good enough, right?*"

"*No, I don't,*" *I snap.*

"*Well you're not. You need to give up.*"

"*No.*"

"*Then come clean, quit cheating.*"

"*I don't cheat!*" *I scream, whirling on him.*

"*Sure, whatever,*" *he says, holding his hands up and backing off a step. Then he walks away, leaving me fuming.*

"*I hate that guy,*" *Tomas says, walking up behind me.*

"*You and me both,*" *I say, turning to greet the mechanic.*

Tomas is always kind and looks out for me when he can.

"*Want I should kick his ass?*"

"*He's not worth it,*" *I observe.*

"*Yeah, you're right. He might bruise my knuckles,*" *Tomas says, holding up his scarred hands.*

"*Thanks though.*"

"*Why don't you report them?*" *he asks, looking at the bruises on my neck.*

"*Because then they win.*"

"*I don't get it.*"

"*If I report them, then it proves they're right, I'm not good enough. I can't make it on my own merit and have to pull rank or go up the chain of command.*"

"*Amara you're the toughest woman I know. Hell, you're the toughest person I know period, no matter the gender.*"

"*Thanks,*" *I say.*

"*I mean it, you need to turn those guys in. They're worthless. Draker at least should be in the brig.*"

"*Ben and I will beat him in the fly off,*" *I say. "That will put him in his place.*"

"*I hope so,*" *Tomas says. "For your sake.*"

"Put who in his place?" Shidan asks.

Opening my eyes, Shidan is looking at me with concern.

"Draker," I mutter. "He's such an ass."

"Oh," he says, placing a cool hand on my forehead then on my cheeks.

He brings the water bottle to my lips which I take, then he pushes a small piece of meat into my mouth.

"Thanks."

"Of course," he says.

I should tell him. I should tell him how I feel. While I can. I don't want him to not know if something happens. I feel like it could happen. It's so hard to focus. My mind keeps wandering. I open my mouth but the words won't come out. I can't admit this to him. What if it makes him do something stupid? What if it gets him hurt?

"Shidan," I say, but it comes out a whisper.

Still he hears it, leaning in close. "Yes, my lyutik?"

"Don't call me that," I exhale, feeling exhausted with the effort of speaking.

Shidan smiles and nods. "Of course, Amara," he says.

"I need to say something." Gathering my strength I push myself to a more upright position.

"What is it Amara? You should rest."

"I think…" I start.

He waits for me to continue but my throat clamps shut.

"Amara, look," Ben says, dropping his fork onto his food tray. "We can't keep going this way."

"Going what way?" I ask, avoiding his eyes.

"You know what I mean," he says.

"No, I don't. Everything is fine just the way it is," I say, shoving another bite of potatoes into my mouth.

Focus on the food. Don't look up, don't meet his eyes, don't let him in.

"You're taking too many risks," he says.

Ben is shaking his head just at the edge of my vision where I refuse to look up. If I look into his eyes, I'll crack. I can't, I won't. No signs of weakness, I have to be strong, no feelings.

"We're fine," I repeat.

"No!" he shouts and the mess hall goes deadly silent.

Every part of me burns feeling their eyes on me. This is what they want, everyone tests us, waiting for a crack. Any sign of weakness in our partnership. Ben and I are the best. Being the best builds resentment in the rest of the crew. Nature of the game.

"We're not okay," Ben whispers, his voice strained. "What you did out there... it's too dangerous. You're pushing too hard. Hell even Tomas says you've taken your fighter beyond the limits of its specs."

Ben rises from the table, picking his tray up. He stands, staring down at me, but I can't look up. Embarrassment keeps me from meeting his eyes. I can't stand seeing the disappointment I know he's feeling. I have been pushing too hard. Trying to one up Draker, keep proving that I'm worthy of the praise heaped on me. It's never enough, but he's right. At some point I'll take it too far.

He's standing right in front of me. Ben is a good-looking guy, damn hot, and could have his choice of women on the ship. If our lives were different, maybe we could be together but they're not. He's my best friend, he'd be the perfect choice for my life but it would complicate things. Complications I can't afford. He's waiting for me to speak, standing too close. My heart pounds in my chest, my throat closes tight. What do I say? Sorry? Hey you're hot? No, better to say nothing.

"Fine," he says. "Just don't do it again, okay? You will get us both killed if you try that maneuver."

Blinking sweat away from my eyes, the med bay comes back into focus. I'm here, right? Shidan strokes my hair, raises the water bottle to my lips again, and waits. He waits patiently with kind eyes, his beautiful face and strong hands caring for me. He cares for me, he loves me and I know it. No matter how much I've tried to deny it I know it.

He loves me and I care about him but is it love? I don't

know. Maybe? I have to tell him. I can't hold this inside, just in case.

"All my life," I say, straining to make my voice louder than a whisper. "I've never been able to... trust. To open myself to someone. I have to be strong. I can't take help because it makes me look weak. They'll use that against me."

"Needing help is not weakness," he interrupts.

I shake my head, placing a hand on his shoulder. He doesn't understand. How can he? No one ever has, and he's an alien from a different culture. What does he know of being a woman in a man's world? Invading enemy territory. Knowing you're not wanted even if you're every bit as good as they are. How hard I pushed for acceptance that would never come. Pushed until it was too late. You can only go so far before it all comes crashing down around you. I can't do that to him.

"In my world, it is. Was," I amend.

Shidan smiles and nods. "Rest my lyutik," he says. "It will all be fine."

The concern on his face is too much. I want to cry in frustration or relief, I'm not sure.

"Okay," I exhale.

I'm tired. So, so tired. It's taking too much effort to keep my eyes open any longer. As they drift shut and darkness welcomes me back, I feel the water bottle at my lips. I drink then I'm drifting...

In my room that night the tears flow free. Having held them back until I was alone, now they won't stop.

Embarrassed, ashamed, and wishing that everything was different than it is. I like Ben, I respect Ben but I can't let Ben be too close. It's hard working so close with him. We're best friends. The Lead/Wingman relationship becomes something more than two people in normal lives ever experience. When your life literally depends on that other person, you can't help but develop feelings for them. Can you? Ben says nothing. Which is fine. It's not just that it's against regulations it's a terrible idea. If I was to do something with Ben, my career would be over.

They'd never look at me as an equal. I'll be what they think I am. The girl who gives 'favors' to get what she wants. Grabbing my screen, I pull up the flight video and play the video again. Ben and I's fighters jet through the black in perfect synchronicity. The engines fire, pushing faster, my body tenses watching the playback, remembering the G-force pressing harder and harder. Then my fighter jerks as I pull back and switch directions in an instant. The force was too much, I blacked out. Ben was matching me, following my lead, and it happened to him too. Our fighters drift aimless in the dark, uncontrolled.

That maneuver can't be done at that speed. My fighter drifts towards Ben's, scraping across his bow. If it had hit a foot back, he'd be dead. My stomach clenches watching it happen again. I've watched it a hundred times, and it never changes. Pulling up the simulator I run it with different variables. The tears run out leaving me empty and dry but I continue working the simulator.

"YES!" I scream leaping off of my bunk.

I found it. The secret, I knew it could be done. Bursting into a run I race across the flight deck towards Ben's bunk. Pounding on his door, impatient for him to open it. Pilots are among the few that have private bunks on the ship. His door slides open and he's standing in a pair of boxers. His muscled body on display, a distinct bulge showing through the loose fabric. He runs his hand through his hair, inadvertently flexing his bicep.

"Amara, what is it?" he asks, blurry eyed, words heavy with sleep.

"I..."

"Yes?" he asks when I don't continue.

"I figured it out," I say.

"What?" he asks, impatient. "And why can't it wait until morning?"

"The maneuver," I say holding the screen out towards him. "We can do it. I know what went wrong."

"Amara, it's too dangerous. We're only here because of luck."

"No, it's not. We have to be good enough," I say, shoving the screen at him again until he takes it at last.

Turning from the door he wanders into his cabin. His fingers dance across it replaying the sim, then doing it again as he sinks into a chair.

"Son of a..." he says, looking up, awe evident on his face.

"Right?" I ask.

He shakes his head side to side. "Yeah," he exhales, staring at the screen. "This could work."

He rises from the seat, still staring at the screen. In slow motion his chin lifts, his eyes rising, until they meet mine. A slow smile spreads across his face.

"I l— ," he starts, his body leaning in towards me.

My eyes widen, my mouth drops open. No! No, you can't say that and I can't feel this. I take a step back.

"No!" I cry, my neck cracking as I jerk awake.

"It's okay, lyutik," Shidan says, pulling me against his strong chest, an arm around my shoulders, his free hand wiping sweat from my forehead with a cloth.

He places water against my lips and I drink it in greedily. Everything hurts. Shidan is only a blur. Blinking rapidly, he finally comes into focus. His strong jaw, beautiful eyes, the concern on his face creates a stabbing pain in my heart.

"I'm sorry," I say, my voice a whisper, anything more taking too much effort.

"No, lyutik," he says. "Do not be sorry. Be well, do not leave me."

"Right," I say, eyes drifting closed against my will. "I'm right here, so… embarrassed."

The word he almost said hangs in the air between us. Ben doesn't say anything, it's so quiet I can hear the hum of the air recycler, feel the vibration of the ship engines through the deck. I'm hyper aware of everything. The slight motion of air moving across the hair on my arms.

Of all the people on the ship, the one man I can't possibly have, the one that would mean the end of my career... has fallen for me.

The ache in my chest grows, my heart refusing to beat, the moment dragging on until I'm sure I'll explode. At least that would be a resolution!

"Right," Ben says, breaking eye contact, his shoulders slumping as he turns away from me.

"Well, we've got the showdown, if you're right, this will put it in the bag for us," he says, pushing the screen at me.

Grabbing it with numb fingers, I nod, swallowing hard but to no avail. My mouth and throat are still dry as a desert.

"Uh-huh," I say, my best attempt at words.

Stepping backwards, unable to look at Ben out of embarrassment, I'm outside his door. He leans against the frame, staring at the floor then nods.

"Great work Amara," he says.

Nodding, I force myself to meet his eyes, not looking away. Pretend it didn't happen. That's the best idea. Nothing to see here, keep moving folks.

The corners of his lips twitch, almost a smile, it's his signature and with his good looks it melts the hearts of any girl he wants. I don't think he ever notices that though. Unlike the other guys on the flight deck, Ben isn't on a mission to sleep his way through every deck of the ship.

"Uh, yeah," I say.

"Early call," he says, nodding. "Don't be late."

"I'm never late!" I exclaim, responding to the button push without thinking.

"Right," he says, his grin splitting his face. "See you then Stancher."

He steps back ,and the door slides shut, ending the moment.

Something soft on my head. That's nice. Eyes, too heavy, open damn it.

Light assaults me as my eyelids slowly crack apart. It feels like they're dragging sandpaper across my eyes. It's painful. Med Bay. Right, here, I'm here. Shidan kisses my forehead. That's what that was. He's humming, a soft sound. I've never heard any of the Zmaj do anything even slightly musical before. It's wordless but very pretty. When he sees my eyes are open he stops.

"Sorry," I croak.

"No, lyutik," he says. "I am sorry. You are perfect."

I shake my head or my best attempt at it that fails mostly because it makes the pounding worse.

"Not... perfect. Don't want... hurt you."

"You will not hurt me, lyutik. I am yours."

"No," I say, struggling to stay here. Already I'm drifting again. "I'll hurt you. Don't want to, you deserve better."

The flight stick in my hand vibrates. Something is off in my ship. I don't know what but I can feel it. The ship is a part of me, an extension of my being. When I bank around to position, it's slight but enough that I'm sure something is wrong. No, that's ridiculous. Tomas went over the ship himself pre-flight. Looking out the window at Ben, I give him a thumbs up as we maneuver our fighters next to each other.

Draker and Jackson move into position at the other end of the generation ship.

"You ready scrub?" Draker asks over my headset.

"I was born ready," I bark.

I look at Ben and can see his grin through his flight helmet. He gives me a thumbs up then flashes his thrusters, wiggling the wings of his fighter side to side in a wave. Show off.

Neither of us have said a word about last night, which is fine with me. It shouldn't have happened. It won't happen again. It can't. It's not just the regs, which a relationship between myself and any of the pilots firmly forbids, it's the changes it would make between us. We depend on each other but as my lead he has to consider the good of the mission first, above all including my life. How could I put that kind of pressure on him?

"Flight Control - we're in position and ready," Draker says over the radio.

"Copy that," Flight Control returns. "Counting down now, good luck."

The count echoes in my helmet. My grip tightens on the flight stick as my thumb hovers over the switch for the thrusters. I look over my instruments making sure, doubts sneaking their way through my thoughts but everything looks good.

"... 2... 1... GO!"

My thumb strokes the switch and the thrusters engage, throwing me back into my seat as the ship jumps from still to two G-force in an instant. The pressure forces me deep into my seat then eases as it normalizes. Ben is slightly in the lead and I'm trailing on his left. Jackson and Draker shot straight up and knowing Draker he'll try to drop in behind us. It's his signature move.

"Apollo, you got eyes on them?" I ask over my headset.

"Negative Stancher," Ben answers.

An alarm flashes on the dash in front of me. Someone has lock on me! I jerk the throttle to the left, opposite of where anyone would think since it leans me in towards Ben but we've practiced this maneuver. He rolls with me like we're one fighter. Light flashes through where my ship just was as I avoid the laser that would have taken me out of the game. The stick shimmies in my hand, again. Something is definitely wrong.

"Roll," Ben orders and my hands comply before I think the thought.

The ship rolls then I dive while Ben breaks up, flipping upside down we both achieve lock on Jackson. A loud screaming sound rips through my cockpit and then Draker's whoop comes over the radio.

He appears out of nowhere, flying between Ben and I with lasers flashing. The fight is on.

"Damn it," I exhale.

So hard to stay awake. The past is a black morass pulling me down into it. The floor is cool so I shift to rest my cheek on it. Shidan isn't here. Where is he? Pushing off the floor, my head explodes with a blinding white pain. I give up, dropping back down with a grunt.

"Lyutik," Shidan says, lifting me off the floor and sitting me back against the wall.

"Sorry," I mutter, unable to force my eyes open. "Shouldn't have slept with you."

"Never say that lyutik," he says, cool hands on my face then water passes my cracked lips. "You are my treasure. We are meant for each other, it is inevitable."

"No," I say, shaking my head but I have to quit, it hurts entirely too much. "Bad... idea. You're better... need better."

"No one is better than you my lyutik," he says.

"Quit... calling me..."

Draker and Jackson are good but Ben and I are the best. We've been battling for most of an hour, neither of us able to get the edge on the other despite multiple target locks on both sides. Those only count for points, we're not playing for points. This is it, the final showdown between us. A final, decisive victory that will settle our rivalry.

"Ready?" Ben crackles over my radio.

"You sure?" I ask, unable to stop the grin spreading across my face.

"Never more," he returns. "Pull him in, Draker's got it bad for you, play bait."

"Done," I say, shifting quickly and spinning while slowing down.

This has to look right, can't be too easy or he'll suspect the trap. Tapping the flight stick I make the bird shimmy, part of the illusion to pull him in and it works. In moments Draker drops in behind me. My systems light up warning he has target lock.

I punch it forward, jumping from one-G to four in an instant. The force pushes me back into my seat, pulling at my skin. My suit pushes back against the force but it's still hard to breathe. Draker follows as I maneuver. I have to make this look good. Tap the stick, shimmy once again, reeling him in.

"Here it comes," Draker gloats over the open channel.

Smiling despite the force pressing against me, I push the flight stick the rest of the way, engaging my full thrusters. The fighter leaps forward adding two more G to the force pushing on me.

"Almost there," Ben whispers over our private comm. "More, let him get closer."

I slow my maneuvering, drawing him in the last bit. The alarm's flashing, target lock, he'll fire any moment. A dot appears ahead on both my radar and out my window. It's coming at me fast. This is it.

"NOW!" Ben yells.

I pull straight back on the flight stick without letting off the thrust. The force increases exponentially as I'm pulled in two directions at once. As I shoot up, breaking in a way that shouldn't be possible, Ben fires. Blackness encroaches on my vision as the force against my body overwhelms the suit's defense against it. My screens light up, flashing, followed by Draker cursing over the open channel.

"No way! You cheated! You can't do that!" he screams.

An alarm sounds and lights flash. The vibration returns in force. The flight stick shakes so hard I have to grip it with both hands to keep it under control. Whatever is wrong with my fighter, it's serious. Pulling back on the thruster, the pressure on me eases and blood returns to my head. My fighter is shaking, hard, working against me.

"Amara," Tomas' voice crackles in my headset. "Amara come in."

"Busy Tomas," I snap.

"Amara, bring it in..." static crackles breaking up his next words. "... dangerous."

"You're breaking up Tomas, come again," I say.

The fighter is fighting me as I struggle to stay in control. Slowing down the thrust more, I let the ship glide, hoping to bring it around and into the landing bay.

".... tampered..." Tomas' voice crackles through a bout of static.

"Amara!" Ben yells over my radio. "What's happening?"

"Something's wrong," I bark. "Fighter is resisting."

"Bring it in," Ben yells.

I'm trying but it's not responding. It shudders then my flight stick goes lax. I'm drifting at high speed. The ship spins, I can't stop it, can't control it. Stars whirl outside my canopy. This is it. The calculations and possibilities race through my mind. They say when you know you're about to die your life flashes before you eyes. All I see is every possible way for me to get out of this situation and end up with nothing. I'm done.

"Amara!" Ben yells.

"It's fine Ben," I say, taking a deep breath. "It's the risk we all take. Sorry about last night."

"No," Ben says, it sounds like he's sobbing over the radio. Not cool Ben, not cool at all.

"Flight Control," I say, flicking over to the open channel. "I'm 99'd."

I give the code for don't rescue.

"Copy that Stancher. All the best Starbuck," Flight Control comes back.

"Starbuck," I snort. "Right, thanks."

The running joke for the inside geeks. I'm the only female pilot so they tease me about my role a lot. The geeks refer to Battlestar Galactica because it pisses me off and they know it.

"Amara," Ben says. "Standby."

"No Ben, don't try it!" I yell at him on the private channel.

I don't know what he's thinking, but whatever it is, it has to be stupid. I'm in a full spin. There's no way to stop me without putting himself in too much danger. It's not worth the risk. We can't afford to lose two pilots with only a slight chance of saving one. It's the wrong decision.

Looking side to side, I try to spot him in the black. Something hits the nose of my fighter, jerking my attention to it.

"Damn it BEN!" *I scream his name.* "Disengage, you damn fool!"

"No can do Amara," *he says.*

He's hooked a magnetic tow line to my fighter. It would work, if I wasn't in an ever increasing spin. The centrifugal force of my spin is just as likely to pull him in, crashing us together in a flaming ball of loss.

Following the line I see his ship. He reverses his thrust and pulls, trying to get me out of the spin. My ship jerks as he does but there's too much force.

"Ben, it's not going to work. I'm spinning too hard. I've got almost no flight control."

"It... will... work," *he says, the whine of his engines over his voice.*

"No, disengage now!"

My ship jerks again but instead of pulling me out of the spin, now I'm flipping head over heel and side to side. The lead line wraps around the nose of my fighter. It's pulling Ben in.

Grabbing the flight stick, I fight against the machine. It bucks and fights but barely responds.

"Almost... got it," *Ben says.*

"Disengage, you idiot," *I say, fighting myself too.*

"No... can... do," *he says.*

He's close, his ship is just outside my window. We will hit, damn it, respond!

My ship bucks, control coming back if only slightly. The nose dips up, opposite the spin but it's too late. My nose cracks up and into Ben's engine. Metal screams against metal, parts flying off, the blue flame of his fighter cuts down into the nose of mine, sputtering as it does. Fuel leaks out of his cracked tanks.

"Ben! Cut the engine! Cut it now!"

His ship jerks to the side, we're eye to eye through our windows. He holds up a hand, pressing it against the glass, he smiles.

"Hey Amara," he says. The line holding us together disconnects ,and he's drifting off now himself. "Just wanted to tell you..."

"What? Cut the damn engine, now!" I scream at him.

His smile shines at me across the growing black between us.

"I love you," he says, then the black is lit up like an exploding star as his ship combusts.

"Can't love you," I say, rousing out of the past. "Can't. Won't hurt you. Won't lose you. No, no, no."

"Shhh," Shidan whispers, comforting me. "It's fine."

"No, not fine," I mutter, cuddling up closer to him. "Damn fool men. Sacrificing idiots. No, not for me. Never again."

18

SHIDAN

*M*oistening a piece of cloth from our dwindling water supply, I dab it across Amara's forehead and cheeks. She's bright red, her lips are cracked, and she's shivering. It's been at least an hour since she last woke up and spoke something coherent. Laying her down onto the floor, I check the monitors.

The pirates are gathering the scavenged things at the main entrance to the broken ship. They're working in teams of two, exploring the remains and carrying back what they find. Two are loading the gathered goods onto their transport. I've waited days but now I'm out of time. Amara is in bad shape. I don't know how much longer she can go without epis and I have to save her.

"Shidan," she mutters.

Moving back to he,r I take her in my arms. She doesn't open her eyes, but it seems to calm her when I'm holding her. I hold the water bottle to her lips and pour a small amount into her mouth. She swallows it at last and I let go of a breath I didn't realize I was holding.

My stomach is a tight knot. Inaction creates a tension in

my muscles that makes me ache to move. I have to get her back to the city. A black fear hides behind every thought as I avoid thinking the one thing that seems most obvious. She will die if she doesn't get epis.

I can't lose her. I won't.

Sliding out from under her, I return to the monitor. I spend the next hour studying the pirate's movements, forming a plan. I have to take them out. There's no way for me to get her out of here unnoticed and if I'm carrying her I won't be able to fight.

"Sacrificing idiots, never again," she mutters.

Going to her side, I kneel and touch her face. She's burning hot. I wet the cloth again and place it across her forehead. She shudders and convulses so I hold her until it passes. I make my decision. I'll save her, no matter what it takes.

I lift and move her to a corner. Moving crates to block her from view if anyone finds a way into the room I then get my lochaber. I give her a drink of water, dampen the towel and place it around her head then I go to the door. I try to work the control panel, entering the same sequence I saw Amara use and eventually I get it open.

A team of two should be deep in the ship. I'll deal with them last, let them come after I've dealt with the ones in the cargo area. As I come closer, I hear the sounds of their guttural language grunting to each other. Flattening myself against the wall I ease my way to the corner then peek around.

There are three of them in a small huddle. Damn it I wanted to catch them apart. Crouching down I pull back and wait, listening. Sounds of shifting boxes then footsteps echo away. I sneak a peek and see one of them carrying a box towards the transport. Good. I count to ten then take a deep breath.

Leaping around the corner with my lochaber over my head I rush towards the two pirates that remain. One of them sees me and grunts, pulling his weapon even as his eyes widen and he tries to point with his other hand. The man next to him grunts but I'm on them before he can turn around.

Swinging my lochaber in a circle over my head I bring it down on the arm raising the weapon towards me. The blade hits the pirate's armor and glances off but it knocks the weapon from his hand. The gun clatters across the floor as the pirate cries out in pain.

I bring the haft of my lochaber up in an uppercut into the pirate's chin. His head snaps back as the sound of crushing bones fills the air. The pirate stumbles back then falls. The second pirate has his weapon out and is bringing it to bear. Whirling my lochaber over my head I swing with the bladed side at his head. Something strikes me in the back before I can connect. It throws my swing off, causing it to miss the man's head as I'm pushed forward.

The right side of my body is numb. Switching the lochaber to my left hand I threaten the pirate in front of me while sidestepping, trying to work him between me and whoever just attacked from behind. Another flash of pain hits me in the right side and my muscles convulse.

"AHHH!" I scream, fighting my way past the pain. "Amara!"

Her name gives me strength. I cannot fail her. She needs me. She's vulnerable and counting on me. I will not let her down.

Circling the enemy in front of me, the pair that was deeper in the ship comes into view. Both of them have their weapons drawn and are taking aim. I have to do something fast so I do the only thing that makes sense. I dive for the one closest. My right side refuses to move so I grab him with my left arm. He fights as we lock into a struggle.

His friends don't seem to care. Shots strike around the two of us then one of them hits him. He grunts in surprise and pain. I whirl and struggle to use him as a shield. The other two don't appear to bother aiming, firing random electrical bolts. One of them hits my left leg and I can't stand.

I hold onto the pirate as I fall to the floor, dragging him with me. Struggling, I get an arm around his neck and hook it with my other, choking him. He struggles against me but I don't let go. The other pirates close and in seconds there are four of them with weapons aimed at me. They growl and speak in their guttural language.

"No!" I scream.

Two of them look at each other than shrug. I try to pull the pirate in my arms over to block the shot but I'm too slow. The blaster fires and everything goes black.

19

AMARA

Something's wrong. I know it the instant I wake up. Jerked out of my feverish dreams, a cold dread creeps through my core. Pushing myself up onto an elbow I work my way to a sitting position. Everything hurts. My joints ache, my muscles are sore, my eyes are dry and burning and my parched throat screams for water.

"Shidan?" my voice cracks.

I'm not where I fell asleep. There are crates piled around me, blocking my view of the room. What has he done? I shake my head as I force myself to my feet. I stumble and catch myself on the wall. Damn this sucks. I close my eyes and focus on breathing until the dizziness passes. Once it's gone, I open them and then push myself into an upright position.

I have to move crates to get out of the small box he built around me. It's exhausting and my headache comes back in force as I work my way out. At last, standing on the far side of the boxes, I look around the medical bay. There's no sign of Shidan but that's no surprise. If he was here, he would have answered my calls.

The monitors. Maybe I can catch sight of him. As I make my way over, drifting to avoid the dizziness and keep the nausea under control, certainty grows. I know him. He's doing something stupid. Sure, it's to 'save' me but it's stupid. There are too many of them to fight but I know him. He will try. My heart swells in my chest until I'm sure it will burst and I shake my head.

"Damn it Shidan," I mutter.

He loves me. Loves me more than his own life but he's not stupid. He knew how dangerous it was but he must have decided he had no choice. The worst part is, I think he might be right. My vision is hazy, weaving in and out of focus, my head is pounding, and my mouth is so dry I can't swallow. My stomach is cramping and my muscles cramp too at random moments that make it hard for me to stand up much less walk.

I'm way past the point of simple dehydration, if that's all it was then the water, salt and potassium would ease the symptoms. No, it's clear I'm in withdrawal. I have to have epis. The side effect of taking it, it's addictive. Once your body adjusts to it, you have to have it.

My knees give out and I collapse to the floor. I try to stand but my left calf cramps, causing me to cry out in pain. I clutch it until the ache passes. If I wasn't so dry I'm sure I'd be crying. I guess there are advantages to being dehydrated, no tears, can't show weakness if you have no tears to shed.

Giving up on standing, I crawl towards the security monitors, grabbing a handhold and pulling myself forward until I reach them at last. My heart sinks the moment I see the first monitor. Shidan is fighting with a pirate.

"LOOK OUT!" I try to scream but he can't hear me and my throat is too dry.

Another pirate is behind him. That one fires his weapon and hits him in the side. His arm falls limp, but he continues to fight, pulling the other pirate around. There's more approaching though, drawn to his commotion. It's only a few moments before they have him down on the ground and he's unconscious and captured.

"No, no, no," I say, sick to my stomach as I watch them bind him and throw him against a wall.

They look at each other and talk in their guttural language. Now I have to save him. Damn it, what can I do?

I sit up and wait for the dizziness to pass then stare at the monitor and try to force myself to think. I feel like I've got a thick fog between me and the world making it hard to form a plan. I see them dragging him towards the loading bay area. They stick him to one side and two pirates remain to guard him while the others return to scavenging the ship.

The loading bay. Something about the loading bay. What is it? A thought tickles at the edges of my mind. I can almost remember it. Closing my eyes, I take a deep breath, then relax. I push aside my worry, my fear, my concerns for Shidan and for myself. Empty my thoughts, just like when I'm preparing to launch my fighter. There is nothing but me and my machine. Nothing else matters.

As I find that quiet place I recall something. The loading bay has built in security systems to take care of problems from volatile materials.. There are safety precautions built into the ship to counteract any problem, including one to force live animals into unconsciousness. They had to allow for us to bring aboard livestock from nearby planets we were passing in case there was a catastrophic loss of the food supply on the ship.

"Thank you Tomas for all your useless knowledge," I whisper, opening my eyes with the beginnings of a plan coming together.

This won't be easy. I force my way back to my feet and dig around the medical area, finding supplies of electrolytes.

I down a handful with some water then another. My headache recedes to a dull roar and the sluggishness eases. My muscles are still having random cramps but that's more from the withdrawal I think than from dehydration. Nothing I can do about it.

Feeling at least a little better, I grab the machine bag we came here for. I need to get to the ship's communication system. If my plan's going to work, I'll need to see all the pirates and goad them towards the security system. I plan to fuck their day up.

Deep breath, push off the wall I'm leaning against, then I'm moving. I stack two crates so I can get up to the door out of the med bay. I need to get deeper in the ship. There's a security center a deck up from the medical bay and that's where I've got to go. The door slides open when I punch in my code. I climb through and lower myself to the floor on the opposite side.

Now to get to the deck above or, I guess, beside me since the ship is on its tilted. I creep along the hall, stopping to listen every tenth step. The last thing I can afford is to run into pirates. It also gives me a chance to rest and deal with the cramping of my muscles. My left leg seems to be the worst. It feels weak, like it doesn't want to hold my weight. Stepping carefully to test it before I put my weight on it is slowing me down, but it's better than falling on my face.

Something clangs behind me and I flatten myself to the wall, holding my breath. Watching behind me I push back as far as I can into the wall and wait. Is it one of them? Straining my ears for the slightest sound I wait until my vision edges grey before breathing and decide it was nothing.

I make it to the elevator up to the next deck and pass my hand over the screen. It lights up but the familiar vibration that would show the elevator is coming doesn't happen. I wait for a few minutes but nothing. It was too much to hope that it would work. I try to pry the doors open but I can't get enough of a grip. Looking around, I find a piece of metal sticking out of a wall that looks like it might help.

Leaving the equipment I'm hauling with me I grab the piece of metal and work it back and forth until it snaps off in my hand. Sliding the thinnest part of the bar into the crack of the doors I lean my entire body into it. The doors open an inch but it's enough for me to get more of the bar in. It doesn't take long for me to get it far enough I can squeeze through.

I'm looking down into a square shaft that runs horizontally. The elevators move on an electromagnetic lift system built into the walls of the shaft which also serve as hand and footholds if the ship was in its normal position. I let the bar fall down then grab the equipment bag and lower it as far into the shaft as I can then let it drop. It lands with a dull thud. Now it's my turn. Hanging my legs over the side I take a deep breath then lower myself down.

My feet touch the ground and I'm in the shaft. I can't stand upright so I crawl, grabbing the bag and starting on my way up to the next floor. The shaft is hot and full of stale air making it harder to breathe. If I wasn't so dehydrated, I'm sure I'd be sweating buckets. That I'm not isn't a good thing.

I'm only going up one deck so it doesn't take long. Grabbing the bar I work it into the slit of the door and then pry. It's a lot harder from this side because I can't get a good angle. There's just not enough room but at last I get it open. Lying on my back, panting, I listen to see if my work has brought any unwanted attention. No clue what I'll do if it has. I'm counting on the fact it's a big chunk of the world ship and there aren't very many pirates scavenging it.

Satisfied at last that no one is coming to investigate my commotion I climb to my knees then poke my head out the open door. I look all around and listen for any signs of pirates before I push the equipment bag out then pull myself out after it. Holding my breath as butterflies beat in my stomach I listen once more for any sounds.

No one comes and I hear nothing. Standing, I take a moment to get my bearings then I head for the security center. I arrive without incident and the door opens. I climb through then shut it behind me. No point in making it obvious where I'm at.

Dominating the center of the room is a massive desk with multiple stations. Each has its own set of monitors and inputs. The entire ship is visible from here. Control of the ship systems is also here. I have to wonder how the engineers, who had thought of everything else, didn't think about us being boarded by space pirates. It seems an obvious threat, at least in hindsight.

Shaking my head, I go to one terminal. My code doesn't work, access denied. Damn it. I hadn't counted on that though I should have. I'm a fighter pilot, why would my security codes get me access to the security consoles?

"Tomas!" I exclaim.

As an engineer Tomas had had access to everything. One night we got drunk together, and he shared his code with me because he thought it was funny. I remember it because it was so damn nerdy, just like Tomas. I activate the terminal again and it flashes ready for password.

"Help me Obi-wan Kenobi. You're my only hope," I say.

The screen flashes three times then I'm in. I shake my head as I chuckle.

"Tomas, you fan boy."

Okay, now to save Shidan. I sure as hell hope the Force is with me because I will need all the help I can get.

20

SHIDAN

*M*y eyes snap open and I'm awake. I try to move but can't. Try to turn my head but nothing happens. A gag around my mouth makes it hard to breathe. My hearts pound as adrenaline pumps into my body. Muscles tense and I try to move again.

Focus! I admonish myself.

Deep breaths. One, two, three, slow the hearts. Okay, evaluate. I'm numb. My muscles feel sluggish and are not responding as they should. The adrenaline is counteracting that effect but I'm slow. I'm bound, legs and arms, wings and even my tail. These pirates know what they're doing.

My internal assessment done, I turn my attention to the surrounding room. Two pirates are close by with weapons at the ready. They're too far away even if I could move. It takes effort, but the numbness is receding and I'm able to move my head side to side. I see no other guards in the area. I'm near entrance Amara and I came through.

Amara. No sign of her, good. They haven't found her. Thinking of her my hearts jump back into hyperactivity.

Adrenaline pumps through my body and the numbness recedes faster. I struggle against the ropes binding me, trying to find any slack. One pirate looks over at the commotion then stomps towards me.

I stop moving, waiting for him to get closer. He utters guttural commands that mean nothing, waving his weapon towards me.

"No clue what you're saying. You look like a majmun's backside," I goad.

He growls and grunts then takes another step closer and I act. Swinging my bound legs I sweep his feet out from under him. Rolling towards him as he crashes to the ground I come to a stop on top. My limited movement leaves no options so I bounce my body to use my larger size to crush him or knock his head to the ground in a hope he goes unconscious.

He grunts as I knock the wind out of him and his weapon clatters to one side. The other pirate shouts and approaches while the one beneath me gets an arm around my neck and pulls back, cutting off my air. His partner looms in my fading vision as I struggle against the one who has me by the neck.

"Hey! Ugly bastards!" Amara's voice booms, filling the space.

Both of the pirates look around, confused, and the one holding me by my neck eases his grip. I gasp in relief and the gray at the edges of my vision recedes.

"Yeah, you two. You slime sucking scumbags!" Amara yells.

Her voice is loud, too loud, its echoing off the walls. The pirate beneath me pushes me off to the side then gets to his feet, retrieving his weapon on his way. Lying on my side forgotten, I watch as the two pirates look around weapons at their shoulders looking for Amara.

"I'm over here you nutbags," she says.

The pirates move in a search and clear pattern. Well coordinated, they approach the stacks of crates and cover each other as one peers around the corner looking for her, ready for an attack.

"You, yeah, you, I see you walking by that open elevator shaft. You think I'm down there? I'm in the landing bay dumb ass. Why don't you come get me?"

She's here? I wiggle around looking for her but can't see anything around the piles of supplies. Shots fire and my heart leaps to my throat as my stomach clenches into a tight knot. I strain against the ropes binding me. I have to help her. She needs me.

The sound of ammunition tinkles as it hits the floor then they stop firing. Did they hit her? There are no screams. I have to know what is happening. I move across the floor like a baby Zmaj working my way towards the sounds of the weapon fire.

"Is that the best you got?" Amara laughs. "Seriously?"

One pirate barks loudly and I can hear the frustration in his voice even if I don't understand the words. Clanging footsteps run into the room. More pirates join the two that were guarding me. Peering around the corner of a stack of crates I see four of them in a huddle. They speak to each other in rough grunts pointing around.

"Four of you? Against little ol' me? Wow, you guys are the worst. Hey, don't worry your other buddies are on their way. Maybe one of them is smart enough to help you morons."

I can't keep myself from smiling. My lyutik is getting them all together. I don't know what it is but I know she has a plan. A swelling in my chest expands until I'm sure my heart will burst. It overwhelms my fear and concern for her safety. She is brilliant and strong and she is mine.

"This way, that's right," she continues goading.

More pirates come into sight, adding to the huddle then one of them shouts and points behind the group. They all turn and as one fire their weapons. I pull back behind the crate and struggle to flip myself over so I can see what they are firing at. Whatever it is, I can't see.

One pirate shouts and continues shouting until the firing stops. They move forward in a tight formation with guns held at their shoulders in lock step. As they pass my position, I'm helpless. Anger and frustration boil in my guts. One of them is close enough I could grab his leg if I wasn't bound. He's just far enough away I can't bite him or I would try that. Anything to save my lyutik.

They're getting close to the far wall and a door slides open as they approach. They split into two and line up to either side. One of them holds up a hand with two fingers out. He motions then lays the fingers down one at a time. As the last one drops the lead two move through the door, opening fire as they do. The rest of the group follows those two in until the entire group of pirates is in the room. The doors slide shut and the sounds of their muffled screams reaches my ears.

Silence. No sounds, nothing happens. I struggle against the bonds holding me tight. Tensing and relaxing muscles, straining with every ounce of my strength to break my way free. Fear fills my stomach with acid. Is she okay? Where is she? What has happened? My thoughts circle a dark drain that pulls me down. I have to get free, I have to make sure she's okay.

"Having fun?" Amara asks from behind me.

She's here. She's perfect. Light outlines her like a halo. Relief floods me and emotions swell up almost too strong for me to contain. I open my mouth to speak but can't, no sound comes. I smile instead. She kneels beside me and a knife flashes in her hands. As she comes closer, I see she's still not well. She's moving but slowly, her cheeks are sunken and her eyes are hollow. There's a slackness to her skin with a grayish tint.

"Amara," I say, my voice cracking.

She looks up from cutting my bonds and smiles. "Miss me?"

Her voice is music to my ears. I can't speak so I nod. She cuts my bonds and I'm free at last. Sitting up I work blood back into my numb limbs.

"What did you do?" I ask.

"I lured them into a room designed to knock out livestock," she says. "It works on pirates too."

"You are amazing," I laugh.

She shrugs. "It's nothing."

"No, it is so much more than nothing!" I exclaim. "You see? I need you as much as you need me. Our need is mutual, equal, we are partners, mates, lovers, it is our destiny. I knew it the moment I saw you outside that dome. I couldn't even speak to you but I knew. My heart swelled at the sight of you. I knew you were the one that would complete me. I am not whole without you."

Amara smiles and shrugs inhaling a long shaky breath. "Sure," she says half-heartedly. "We should search the pirates for supplies then get back to the city. I don't feel great."

"Of course," I answer, concern filling me and over-whelming my need for her agreement.

I stumble as I climb to my feet. Pins and needles stab at my feet and legs as blood flow returns to normal. Amara stands close while I steady myself on a stack of crates. I roll my shoulders, stretch my arms, and step up and down until my body feels like its back to normal.

"You okay?" she asks.

"Yeah, now." I smile and put an arm around her shoulders.

She stiffens, its subtle but I can't help noticing. She doesn't move away though and we walk to the room the pirates went in. They lie around having dropped in their formation. At first I think they must be dead but when I search the first one I notice he's still breathing.

"They're alive," I say, surprised.

"Yeah, I'm not a killer."

Primal instinct pushes me to finish them. They're a threat and I should take them out. I don't because of her. She didn't kill them, I can't come behind her and do it after she let them live. I take all the weapons I can find and their food supplies.

It doesn't take long for us to search and pile what we find outside the room. I'm searching the last one when there's a crash behind me. Whirling around I see Amara lying on the ground.

"Amara!" I scream, rushing to her side.

Her eyes flutter but she doesn't respond otherwise. Her breathing is shallow, her face flushed. When I check for her heartbeat, it's thready and weak. She needs epis. I only hope that there is some in the pirate's belongings.

The pile of supplies we took off of them isn't that large but there are lots of small cases. I tear through each of them ripping them open and dumping out the contents. I'm almost out of options when one reveals what I seek. Epis. It's fresh too, fresh enough anyway, it still has its luminescent glow. I run back to her side and kneel. Tearing off a piece of the plant I push it past her parched lips. She mutters something unintelligible but instinct takes over and she chews.

I hold her head in my lap and wait for her to swallow. I tear small pieces of it off and feed them to her. It takes time but her fever drops, her eyelids quit fluttering, and color returns to her skin. As I feed her, the last piece of epis she jerks and her eyes open. She sits up quickly and gasps in air.

"Damn it," she curses.

"What my lyutik?"

She looks over her shoulder and glares at me. Her expression softens then a half smile plays around her lips. "Come here," she says.

She wraps her arms around my neck and pulls me into a kiss. Heaven couldn't taste any sweeter.

AMARA

We have time, just enough, I think as I kiss Shidan and pull him closer. The pirates will be out for hours and we're safe and together. I care about him, more than I've ever cared about anyone in my life. I need to show him and I don't know how else to do it.

His hands run along my legs. I shift around until I'm sitting on his lap. His hard cock strains against his pants. I like the way it feels as it presses against my clit. His tongue pierces my lips like an invader come to claim.

I care about him. Is it love? Butterflies dance in my stomach, my heart is racing, it's more than desire or lust, but what is it? Running my fingers along the gorgeous lines of his face I love the cool, slight roughness of his scales. It's almost like a five o'clock shadow on a man, a stubble, rough on the fingers, but so damn sexy. Grinding my hips against him elicits a soft moan into our kiss.

I love the sounds he makes. The way he moves. The way he looks. I love the way he cares for me, no matter what I say or do. Is that love?

His hands work their way under my shirt to my breasts and my nipples harden. I wrap my arms around his neck and grind against his bulge. Now I'm moaning. It's hard to think past the sensations of the moment.

I know I have to decide but not now. Wetness is soaking the thin cloth separating us and I need him. He pulls my shirt over my head then his hot mouth is on my nipple. Shidan slips a hand down my pants and presses against my pussy, moving his hand in a circle causing a shiver up my spine. He lifts me up with one hand without letting our lips part.

As he moves his hand back and forth I lean my head back and cry out my pleasure. "Shidan!"

When he lowers me down his cock is against my opening, sliding into my wetness to the first ridge. He's so big it pushes my body to the limit. No matter how many times we have sex this moment always drives me over the edge. He pushes in and I groan. The sense of fullness, of pushing the limits of my body, brings me a euphoria of joy.

He wants me to be his, yet I hold back. He penetrates my body but part of me I keep separate. Why? Why can't I let him in?

He's deep and I rotate my hips as he thrusts. I ball my fists into the hair at the back of his neck and press my forehead to his, grinding on top of him as he pistons. I ride the base ridge of his cock until I can't breathe, I hold it, every muscle of my body tensing. I cling to him as his hips pound and another scream rips from my throat. I press my clit as hard as I can, inhaling at the same time I move my head back, thrusting my breasts into Shidan's face.

Knowing what I need he suckles and I groan. I rotate my hips on his cock as hard and as fast as I can. I pant with the need for release.

"Shidan, Shidan, yes, oh god yes!"

My orgasm stalks me, coming ever closer.

Somehow I thrust faster, and he grips my ass, pulling me in even tighter against his cock. The pressure is beautiful and I arch my head back, grinding and rotating.

"I'm going to come, my lyutik!" Shidan groans.

Just then shudders run along my body and my pussy convulses, orgasm coming in waves. I lean forward, holding on to his bottom lip with my teeth as together we find release.

It passes at last and I inhale a deep breath. Opening my eyes, I look into his. They're beautiful.

His cock softens inside me and then he grabs me by my waist, lifts me up, and then lowers me back down. His second cock is ready. I'm wet and willing. His cock glides in and I'm swept away. He pistons, I don't know how long we move. He thrusts in and I lift. His huge cock is insatiable. He takes me, claiming me as his and in the throes of passion I give myself over. I could love him. It might be okay.

He pushes deep and holds. "Amara!" he cries out, almost driving me over the edge.

The deep rumble of his voice is sexy. He saved me but I also saved him. He's right in that we need each other. Can I be strong while needing him? Is it possible to have both?

He slides his legs out from under himself then he's over me, penetrating and driving in. He lowers until our lips meet while his hips thrust. We kiss, I'm finding my way. Maybe I can love him. Maybe it won't cost me everything.

My fingers touch his soft, membranous wings. They shift at my touch and it strikes me how alien he is. How strange it is that in all my years on the ship no man, no human, ever got this close. None of them could penetrate my shields. He drives through them like his cock driving into my pussy. Straight to my core.

The coiled spring tightens and I'm about to come again. It hits me out of nowhere, grabbing my body and taking over.

Waves of pleasure wash through me like the surf pounding the beach. Relentless, unending, coming again and again. I'm overwhelmed by the sensations. Driven to places I've never been. My legs lock around his waist holding him deep.

It's clear I have to explain it all to him.

22

SHIDAN

*T*he epis worked. Amara moves easily, and she appears to be in full health again. My heart swells with joy and love watching her dress. She is mine. I am hers. Life is as it should be. Now we must return to the city with the technology we found.

"Grab that bag over there," she orders.

I do so. I don't know which pieces are important and which are not.

"What are we going to do about the pirates?" I ask.

Amara frowns, a small wrinkle forming between her eyebrows. I think it's sexy when she does that. I don't point it out to her as I know she does not agree. She thinks it's a flaw. If only she could see herself as I see her. Perfect.

"I don't know," she says.

I nod. Killing in cold blood is not the Zmaj way but they are too dangerous to leave as they are. A threat to us, our friends, and our families.

"I will take care of it," I say.

She protests but then her shoulders slump and she nods. I leave her to gather the supplies.

When I walk in the room, none of the pirates are stirring. Staring at them, my first impulse is to eliminate the threat, but that is just too wrong. It goes against everything I am. A warrior does not strike down an unconscious foe. However, I cannot leave this threat without handling it.

I smile as an idea occurs. They are a threat because of their equipment, not their skills. I will deprive them of that.

Stripping each of the pirates is a lot of work. Their armor is intricate and well made. Once I figure out the first one, though, the rest go faster.

"What are you doing?" Amara asks from the doorway.

"Handling the problem."

She stares at what I've done then a smile breaks out on her face. "Need help?" she asks.

"This is the last one. Do you know how to operate their vehicle? If not we must make sure it's disabled."

"I'm sure I can figure it out."

"Good, that will speed our journey home."

"I'll go look it over," she says, turning and walking away. She stops a few steps beyond the door and turns back, "Shidan?"

"Yes?"

"Good job," she says, then turns and walks away.

My hearts swell in my chest. It's more than a compliment, it's a door opening. A door she always keeps closed but I see the crack. I couldn't be happier as I finish up. I strip the last of the pirates and move him to the pile of naked aliens I've created in the corner.

When Amara returns, I'll have her seal this door. They will have every opportunity to survive but using only their wits. Their weapons and armor will come with us. I gather an armload of the stripped equipment and head out to their transport. As I approach the transport it rumbles, then lifts into the air a foot off the ground expelling a cloud of sand and dust. My extra lids close, protecting my eyes but I get a mouthful of sand. Coughing, I drop one armload of equipment to wave the sand out of my face. When I can see again Amara is standing in the open doorway of the transport, grinning.

"Sorry about that," she says. "I figured it out."

"Good my lyutik," I say as I retrieve the dropped gear.

The transport is almost full of scavenged crates. Once I've added all the gear I took from them, there is no room for more.

"We have the medical equipment?" I ask.

"Yes, it's over there. Thanks to this I was able to get some extra stuff that might be helpful."

"Ah, good."

"Let's get out of here," she says as she leads the way into the transport machine.

She walks through a door and I follow. There's a small space with two seats that look out a large window. Dials, buttons, switches, and sticks cover the panel in front of the chairs. Amara slides into the seat on the left and motions I should take the one on the right.

Her fingers move over the dashboard, flipping, pushing, and otherwise working the equipment in some arcane magic. Sounds respond to her actions. I hear the door we loaded the equipment in close then with a sudden jerk the machine jumps forward and we're moving. I grab the arm of my seat and reach out for her which makes Amara laugh.

"It's fine," she assures me.

I nod and force myself to at least appear relaxed for her sake. My seat vibrates, the machine rumbles, things shake that seem like they should not be. I've never traveled inside a machine before and I don't like it. My stomach is a tight knot. Looking out the window ahead things are flying at us too fast. Amara moves the stick in front of her side to side and the machine responds by turning in the direction she wants.

It doesn't ease my nerves. Boulders fly at us but she dodges. Some objects we hit and bounce over tossing us out of our seats then we slam back down. The seats have a high back making it impossible for me to sit in mine which is making the ride worse. My tail and wings have no place to go so I sit on the edge.

"Do we have to go so fast?" I ask.

"Why not?" Amara laughs, enjoying herself.

Her face is alight with joy. She maneuvers the transport with a deft touch. The delight in her eyes is something I've never seen before. The way her hands move across the board in front of her is amazing. There are so many things happening I don't understand. She's at home and it shows. I bounce out of my seat and hit my head on the ceiling.

"Oops," Amara laughs as I land in a heap, half on my seat.

"Oops?" I ask, annoyed. "This thing is trying to kill us. We need to get out and walk. Send someone else to get this monster."

"Oh calm down," she says. "I over sped up around that dune back there," she waves a hand dismissively. "Still getting used to the reaction time."

I glare while rubbing my head. She may be having fun but I'm miserable. The knot in my stomach gives way to a wave of nausea as I move back onto my seat. Closing my eyes makes it worse. I can feel the motion happening around me. I focus on breathing and holding myself in the seat.

She is right though. It's not long before the rough turns and the bouncing settles down and we're traveling back to the city more quickly than I ever thought possible. I've never moved this fast before. The suns are barely setting when I see the dome of the city glittering in the distance.

"That's amazing," I say.

Amara grins at me. "Like that, huh?"

"Three days travel done in one? I could get used to that!"

"Yeah, but this transport is almost out of fuel."

A few moments later the machine jerks, shakes, then comes to a stop, thudding down to the ground.

"What happened?" I ask.

"Out of fuel," she says.

"Oh," I say as disappointment wells up.

"Well that's all she wrote folks, we made it most of the way though," Amara says, uncharacteristically chipper.

She leads the way back into the cargo area and I follow as she digs around the crates until she finds the large bag with the medical machine. Hefting it to her shoulder I step forward and take it from her as she turns. She looks ready to argue but then something in her eyes softens and she nods, letting me have it.

She opens the door and we walk across the desert. It's not far at all to the city. We're close enough I can see people are gathering at the airlock. The suns are dropping below the horizon casting long shadows when we reach it. Once we're in, I find Rosalind and Sverre standing side by side. They look stern. The other humans gathered around them are talking amongst themselves, pointing out at the transport.

"Looks like you had an adventure," Rosalind says, looking us over.

"You could say that," Amara answers.

"Did you find it?" Rosalind asks.

"Yeah and a lot more," Amara says, hooking her thumb over her shoulder at the transport. "I don't know what all is out there but it's loaded."

"I'll take charge of getting it unloaded," Gershom says, pushing his way through the crowd.

A hiss slips out before I can stop it. The bijass threatens to consume my thoughts as the desire to harm him rears its head. Amara touches my arm. A soft, gentle touch, but it pulls all my attention back. She shakes her head and smiles at me driving the bijass away. Silent, I nod, and her hand drifts down my arm to take my hand in hers.

"Fine," Rosalind says. "Bring everything to the warehouse. We'll sort it out there."

"Absolutely," Gershom smiles and nods.

There is something about him I don't like or trust. He's wrong, off somehow, and it goes beyond his blatant dislike of my race. He makes my scales itch.

"We need to go set this up," Amara says, pointing at the bag I'm carrying.

"Right," Rosalind agrees. "Let's go."

The sound of Gershom barking orders fades behind us as we make our way through the city. Glancing over my shoulder I see him organizing people into small teams. There's something more there than meets the eye, if only I could put my finger on it.

"How is Calista?" Amara asks as we turn a corner and I lose sight of Gershom.

"Rough but okay," Rosalind says.

"Good," Amara says. "Well we're back. This should help."

"What happened out there? We worried when you didn't return on time."

"Pirates," I say.

"How many?" Rosalind asks.

"Eight that we know of," Amara answers. "We knocked them out and took their weapons and armor."

Rosalind nods. "And their transport?"

"Yeah," Amara grins. "Ain't it great?"

"Until they come to collect," Rosalind says.

Amara frowns.

"We must be ready," I say.

We arrive at our destination and Amara goes to work on setting up the machine. It mounts onto one bed. I hold parts and hand her wires as she works. At last she steps back.

"Well, here goes nothing," she says as she reaches over and flips a switch.

A series of lights flash, red, then blue, then green. A screen lights up, flashes three times, then symbols appear. The machine beeps and then two metal arms on its side rise and wave around the air. I take a step back, pushing Amara behind me and lower to a crouch, ready to attack.

"Don't be silly," Amara says, pushing past me.

She walks up to the bed and the two arms turn and point at her. The ends of the arms are small cylinders. A blue light comes out of both of them then they move down the length of Amara. The machine makes a whirring noise, beeps several times as the lights flash different colors then it whistles and something else flashes on the screen. It brightens and then it projects an image out over the bed.

A tiny body, a baby, floats in the air over the bed. It turns in a slow circle. The tiny body is no bigger than my pinky finger, curled into a tight ball. I move closer to look at it, standing behind Amara.

"No," Amara says. "It can't be."

"What is it? Is the machine not working?" I ask.

"No. It can't be! It's broken, damn thing must be, that's what it has to be!"

"I don't under-"

"Stop!" she screams, whirling around and pushing me back.

"Amara what is— "

"It's not possible"

189

She shakes her head as tears form in the corners of her eyes. Her hands ball into fists then she storms past me and runs out of the room. I want to follow her. I want to run after her but I know it will only make her more angry. Indecision locks me in place.

I turn and look at the small hologram projected over the bed and contemplate what it means.

23

AMARA

*I*t can't be. I'm not ready for this. I just decided to let him in and now this? How did this happen?

What am I saying, I know damn well how it happened! I'm a fool. I've done this to myself. I can't do this. Can I? Cold chills run over my skin. Walking the streets in the hot outside air should warm me but it can't touch the chill. I don't even know how long I've been out here, wandering in a circle, trying to wrap my head around the situation.

Wrapping my arms around my stomach it hits me. There's life inside, growing in me. Closing my arms around it, a warm glow spreads from my core out through my limbs. It combats the fear. One or the other will have to win out sooner or later.

"Amara!" Mei's yell pulls me out of my thoughts.

"What?" I ask, startled as I whirl around.

It takes a moment to spot her. I've been so lost in my thoughts, I don't know where I'm at. She's at the door to the medical building, smiling. Her beautiful, long blond hair looks like a red halo in the dim light of the setting suns. Having gotten my bearings I walk towards her.

"It's time! Calista is in labor!"

"Damn."

We run through the building. The rest of the girls stand in a huddle as Mei and I arrive. Sverre and Astarot stand a few feet to one side, talking softly to each other.

"What are we waiting for?" Mei asks, rushing past the group and through the door to the medical area.

Calista is on the bed already panting, sweat pouring down her face. Jolie, swollen belly, and all, is next to her wiping her forehead with a damp cloth and making soft sounds. Calista's hands grip the rails of the bed as she pants faster and her jaw tightens.

"MMMMHHH," she groans then returns to panting.

"How far apart?" Mei asks, moving to the side of Calista opposite Jolie.

"Less than one minute," Jolie says.

"This machine isn't helping!" Ladon hisses.

Somehow I'd missed him standing in the shadows at the head of the bed.

"It will," I say.

"It had better," he hisses, the threat obvious in his voice and his words.

"Okay Calista, it's time," Mei says, placing a hand on Calista's face. "I will get you in position."

Mei motions at us girls but I hang back. The look on Calista's face is pure agony, twisted into a harsh grin that is a parody of amusement. My stomach clenches seeing her go from panting heavily to gritting her teeth and groaning.

The other girls move to either side like they've practiced for this moment. They take Calista's pants off, pushing her legs up to an angle. The machine arms move around her and blue lights shine onto her protruding stomach. Fear makes a cold sweat across my skin seeing her like this. I can't do this. How can she? How is she bearing this much pain?

A hologram of a baby appears above the bed. Mei looks from it to Calista and places a hand on the laboring woman's stomach, feeling around. She presses a spot on Calista's side and the hologram baby's head moves.

"It's not quite head down yet," Mei says.

"That's not good, right?" Lana asks.

"No, it's not," Mei frowns.

"Help her!" Ladon yells, his wings fluttering and his tail swinging from side to side so hard and fast that Inga has to dodge to avoid being knocked to the ground.

"Ladon!" Mei yells.

Ladon turns towards her, rage on his face. He hisses as his hands curl, showing sharp nails ready to attack.

I'm watching all of this happen in slow motion. Ladon is losing it. It's obvious. He's giving in because Calista is in pain and he can't fix it. His love for her is too strong. Too much for him to bear her being hurt. It's making him dangerous. He pushes Inga to one side then Lana is in his way and he shoves her aside too as he heads for Mei.

Rosalind moves but she won't make it in time. I move, thrusting myself between Ladon and Mei.

"Stop!" I say, putting a hand on his chest.

I can feel his hearts pounding as his chest rises and falls with ragged breaths.

"Out of my way human," he hisses.

"No," I say, standing straight and pushing him back. "You love her, we get it, but this is women's work. You have no place here, now get out."

"I'll not— "

"You will do what I say!" I yell, pointing at the door. "Out! Now!"

He hisses, his wings open wide and his tail makes violent slashes side to side but he doesn't move forward. Meeting his glare, I wait him out. Ladon's wings fold to his back, his tail calms, then his arms drop to his side.

"I'll— " he starts.

"No, you won't," I cut him off. "Out. Now."

He hangs his head then turns and walks out of the room without another word. Everyone lets out a collective sigh of relief as he leaves.

"Wow," Mei says, looking at me in awe.

"It's nothing," I say. "Let's do this."

Mei nods and while watching the machine and murmuring words of encouragement to Calista she gently presses on her stomach. The hologram shifts and all the girls in the room release a collective breath.

"The baby is in position!" Mei exclaims.

"Good, good, good, good," Calista pants like a mantra.

"Okay, we're almost ready, when the next contraction hits, you push okay?"

"Yes, yes, yes," Calista nods, sweat pouring down her face then it hits. Her face twists in pain. She cries out, a wordless sound as she groans.

When I look at Calista again, I see more than I did before. I don't just see pain and the agony. There's something much more now that I look with eyes not clouded by fear. The panting between pushes is her focusing, preparing herself. The pushes are concentration, intense sure, but concentration. She's in a zone, she's creating life. Life may begin in pain and blood but it's still a miracle she's creating.

As I realize this my heart explodes in my chest with feelings and emotions too strong. My arms wrap around my stomach and I embrace the life growing inside of me.

It doesn't take long before the strong cries of a new life emerge. Mei lifts the baby up and places it against Calista's chest. Inga moves closer, laying a blanket across mama and newborn.

The baby suckles while we all move closer to watch. It's the most beautiful, heart wrenching, perfect moment I've ever seen.

"Look at his eyes," Lana whispers.

"They're beautiful," Inga says.

"Those scales!" Rosalind says, a softness in her voice I've never heard before.

Calista is glowing in a way I've never seen. She smiles and coos at the baby in her arms. Jolie has tears streaming down her face with her hands crossed over her large belly. I place a hand on my stomach, eyes swimming with unshed moisture.

The baby's tiny hands clutch at the air as he suckles. His perfect, round face is lightly mottled with brilliantly colored scales. He stretches and kicks until his little feet peek out from under the blanket. The tears finally fall down my face as I watch. I can do this.

"Okay, I handled the umbilical cord, and the afterbirth came easily while he nursed," Mei says with a smile.

After a while, the newborn's suckles slow.

"Can I wash him now?" Mei asks.

Calista breaks his seal with a finger then holds him up. Mei takes him and Calista lays back into her pillows, sighing. I follow Mei to the counter where she unwraps the baby. He coos and makes soft hissing sounds. Mei lays the blanket aside the lowers him into the warm bath prepared for him. As she does I get my first good look at the baby.

He's covered in bright scales, brilliant shades of yellow, blue, and green. His eyes are slit like his father's and yellowish green. His wings are gorgeous! Tiny, translucent, and shimmery. They're still folded firmly to his back, covered in birth. His tail is a tiny little nub that wiggles back-and-forth splashing at the water. Tears well up in my eyes and I struggle to not break down and ball. He's so beautiful, so perfect, it's overwhelming. I need to talk to Shidan.

"Amazing," Inga says, coming to stand next to me.

She wipes a tear from her cheek, smiling from ear to ear.

"Yeah," I agree, unable to say more because emotions close my throat.

He is amazing. His tiny little fingers, little toes, that tail, and the wings! So perfect, so small, so much I can't process. So much feeling at one time. Inga puts an arm around me and pulls me close. Feeling out of character for myself I return her embrace as we watch Mei wash the baby.

"We should let Ladon know," I say.

Inga nods but we stand together until Mei finishes bathing the baby. She takes vitals before returning him to Calista who puts him back to her breast where he latches on and nurses.

"Have you guys picked a name yet?" Inga asks.

Calista giggles and strokes the baby's cheek. "Illadon."

"Illidan, like hero of Azeroth Illidan?" Jolie's look of amazement is priceless.

"Only sort of! Il-la-don," Calista sounds it out. "It's like naming the baby after his daddy but more awesome!"

"Calista, you are the biggest nerd ever and I love you!" Jolie laughs.

"I think it's the perfect name for a new, ferocious little warrior," Inga insists and the baby coos like he agrees.

My jaw hurts I'm smiling so much as I head out to tell the men they can come meet our newest community member.

I also have to find Shidan.

I can't keep holding back from him forever.

24

SHIDAN

"*I*'m at a loss," I say.

"You told her how you felt?" Astarot asks.

"Yes."

"And she didn't respond in kind?"

"No," I say. "I think we're close. She lets me in but then pushes me away. She is my treasure. I want to protect her and cherish her."

"I understand," Sverre says.

"Well, there's only one thing to do," Astarot says.

"What is that?" I ask.

"Tell her. Again. Lay it all out for her. Make it clear to her you don't want to take anything from her but to give her everything. She seems as if she is a strong woman who doesn't want to lose her identity. I've seen you two together. This is what she fears."

I nod my agreement. He's right. I see it.

"The whole is greater than the sum of its parts, this is the power of love," Sverre says.

Ladon punches the wall, interrupting our conversation. We all look to see if he's okay. He has resumed pacing back and forth, hissing, his tail slashing violently from side to side, wings rustling. We exchange a look, wondering which of us should go to him. Approaching a Zmaj that close to being in the grip of the bijass isn't easy. Sverre shrugs, accepting the responsibility and goes to Ladon.

Sverre approach slowly, his hands held out before him. Ladon stops pacing and glares. The two of them having pregnant women creates a connection. It must be strong enough to fight back the bijass as Ladon doesn't attack Sverre. It hasn't been that long since Ladon was kicked out of the birthing room, but I imagine for him each passing moment drags like entire marks of the suns.

Empathy wells in my gut. Unsure if his woman, his treasure is okay, or if his child is here. Have there been complications? Are they both well? Imagining how powerless he must feel right now creates an ill feeling in my stomach. How would I react if Amara was in there?

Sverre places a hand on Ladon's shoulder and talks to him softly. I can't hear the words but in a few moments Ladon relaxes and nods. The two of them pace back and forth together. The immediate threat of Ladon losing control to his bijass passes and I return to my own thoughts.

"Well?" Astarot asks.

"Well what?" I ask.

"Are you going to do it?"

I don't answer him immediately. Do I tell her? Putting her on the spot in front of others could be bad. It might backfire. She's pregnant, with our child. I know that's what the machine was saying. I need the commitment between us. I need to feel she accepts me and is ready to create a life together with me.

"I…" I want to say yes but I can't. What if she says no?

"But?" Astarot asks.

"What if she denies me?"

"Will you give up then?"

"No."

"Will you walk away from her?"

"No."

"So tell me, what do you have to lose?"

There is wisdom in his words. The door to the delivery room opens and Jolie is there. Her face glows but tears stream down her face. Her smile spreads across her face wider than I've ever seen. Ladon is next to her so fast I don't see him move, leaving Sverre standing on his own.

"It's a boy!" she says. "Come, come see Illadon!"

Ladon is through the door before she finishes speaking. The rest of us follow. Trepidation makes my scales itch. I shift my wings creating a soft fluttering sound then take a deep breath before I walk through the door behind Astarot.

Calista lies on the bed with the new baby at her breasts. Her hair is matted to her head but there is a beautiful glow to her face I've never seen before. It's stunning. She looks beautiful, filled with life, and powerful. Ladon is next to her, leaning down to be close. He kisses her forehead, resting his head against hers while staring down at the tiny life in her arms.

Sverre is with Jolie while Astarot and I stand off to one side in awkward silence. Amara is on the far side of the room from me, not far from the bed with Inga, Lana, and Rosalind. Mei is moving around doing something with the machines that helped with the birthing.

The baby takes my breath away. He's so tiny. I've never seen a baby before in my life and did not understand one would be so small. His little hand clutches for a hold on the blanket, letting me see his fingers. They're perfect with the smallest nails, wrinkled fingers each one so flawless. Out of the corner of my eye I see Amara and I'm drawn to her stomach. In there is our child, growing. Our child, which will be small, defenseless, dependent on her and I for everything.

Meeting Amara's eyes for the first time I see tears. My heart breaks at the sight and I want to run to her, to destroy whatever is causing her pain, but in that instant I realize they are tears of joy. I understand as I feel almost the same. Hope fills the room, a joyous feeling that pervades everything. A buoyancy that is so new, so different, it lifts my spirits and fills me with wonder at the possibilities of the future.

"Go to her," Astarot whispers, pulling my attention to him.

When I look over I see he's not staring at the baby but at the other females. Following his gaze it strikes me who he's looking at.

"Her?" I ask, keeping my voice soft. "She's your one?"

He starts as his eyes dart back. "What are you talking about?" he hisses.

I smile, knowing I found his secret. I will keep it for him but I know. I know what he is experiencing. In some odd way it makes me feel a kinship to him.

"Go handle your own affairs," he growls.

"Of course," I say.

I close my eyes and inhale, filling my lungs with clean air then let it out slowly. When I open my eyes, I brace myself then walk over to the human females. They watch my approach and it's like they're waiting to see if I'm a threat before they stampede. Doubt creeps in but I push it aside. Amara watches me closest of all, I can't read the look on her face. It doesn't make my task easier but then nothing with her is easy. It doesn't matter because she's worth it.

"Amara," I say.

She looks up and swallows. Her eyes blink several times then she looks away and wipes away a tear. "Yeah?"

"I need to tell you something."

Her face flushes pink, and she looks at the surrounding girls. "Okay," she says at last.

I take the moment to gather my thoughts. There's a smacking sound as the baby pulls away from Calista's breast. I glance over and see she and Ladon are both watching.

"I love you Amara. I have from the moment I first laid eyes on you. I cannot imagine my life without you in it. You are the suns in my universe. You burn bright and beautiful and I want to embrace you and hold forever."

"Shidan— "

I hold up my hand and shake my head. "Please, let me finish," I say, and she purses her lips then nods. "It's more too. I need you. I need you because together we are stronger, better than we are apart. I have never known this feeling. I have never known love. When the devastation happened, I was a child. I was alone, but I learned to survive. I don't want to be on my own any longer. I don't want a world you are not a part of. You are the most amazing person I've ever met."

I lower myself to my knees in front of her and take her hand. "Amara," I continue. "Will you be my treasure, my love, and my mate?"

Tears run down her face. She wipes at them with furious motions. My hearts pound so hard I'm unsure how they don't explode out of my chest. They roar in my ears. My hand holding hers trembles as I wait for an answer. The room is silent as if everyone is holding their breath.

The moment drags on. I can't breathe. I can't blink. Anticipation builds until I'm sure I've fallen into some stuck moment in time that will never end.

"Yes," she says, her voice cracking on the single word.

A weakness runs up my spine and I almost fall over with relief. My hearts beat even faster as I leap up and sweep her into my arms, twirling her as our lips crash together with bruising force. Her tears flow as we kiss. There's the sound of applause and people laughing then there are arms around us pulling us into an embrace.

I set her down on her feet at last. The women have gathered in a circle holding the two of us. All of them have tears and laughter. Joy expands my chest. I've never felt so much happiness. I can't contain it. Laughter breaks out of me and then I can't stop. I have to have the release.

"Congratulations!" "I'm so happy for you!" "Totes jealous, girl!" The girls' words are a blur.

From across Calista's bed, Astarot is grinning from ear to ear. He was right. I gambled it all, and it worked. I turn into Amara, holding both her hands and losing myself in her beautiful eyes.

"I love you," I say, loud enough for everyone to hear. "Always."

"I love you too," she says, rising to kiss me.

The sounds of oohs and ahhs surround us. Everything is perfect.

"We really need to talk," Amara whispers against my shoulder.

25

AMARA

I can't believe he did that. In front of all these people. What if I'd said no? He's brave, so damn brave, it's one of the things I admire in him and yes, I have to admit it; I love him.

It's okay. I can love him. He needs me as much as I need him. Just like on the ship fighting the pirates. It took both of us. One alone wouldn't have been able to do it. I don't know why it took me so long to get it.

It took both of us. Raising this baby will take both of us too. No way I can face a future of caring for a tiny life alone. I haven't told anyone else yet about the baby. I haven't come to terms with it yet. Looking at the baby in Calista's arms, a warmth spreads out from my stomach. Shidan's arm around my shoulder hugs me tight to his side. It opens me up in ways I've never felt before. His heart beat pulses into my side, strong and stable, and I feel my own heart pacing his. This is what love is. I know it, now.

Illadon is looking around the room, smiling and cooing. He locks eyes with me. His beautiful, gold flecked, greenish eyes with their dragon slits look just like Ladon.

"Congratulations," Inga says, pulling me into an embrace.

"Thank you," I say as I return her hug.

Shidan leans down close, nuzzling and kissing my neck.

"I'm so happy for you," Mei says as she comes over and hugs me then Shidan.

Lana comes up next and hugs me. As she embraces Shidan, in her low cut shirt and skin tight pants, a stab of jealousy drives into my heart taking me by surprise. I've never felt it before but once I recognize it for what it is I know it's ridiculous. Lana is my friend. Her natural flirtatious nature is just the way she is.

"You deserve this," Lana says as she walks away and I smile.

As everyone's attention returns to Lana and the baby. Shidan and I stand back, holding hands.

"It's time to let them rest," Mei says as the day grows late.

No one wants to leave but everyone says their goodbyes one at a time until Shidan and I are the last ones. I walk over to the bed and lean down to hug Calista.

"I know," she whispers.

"What?" I ask in surprise.

She doesn't answer me but puts a hand on my belly.

"How?" I ask, my eyes widening in surprise.

Calista just smiles.

"Tell no one," I insist.

"I won't," she agrees. "How long?"

"Not long," I say and Calista nods but her brow furrows with concern. "It's okay."

Somehow her words fill me with relief from a tension I didn't know was still there. She's been there, she's done this. I know women have been giving birth since the dawn of time but that's human babies. Giving birth to a hybrid, alien-dragon baby is a little more overwhelming. Reassurance from the first woman to do it goes a long way.

She kisses my cheek as we embrace once more then Shidan and I take our leave. We walk in silence towards my apartment, holding hands. We're comfortable, relaxed and natural. We make our way through the city as I think about logistics of our future. Where will we live? What preparations do we have to make for the baby?

Eventually we find ourselves outside the small building Shidan has been using as a home. He kisses me, then in a single motion sweeps me off my feet, carrying me through the door and pushing it closed. He takes me straight to the bed where he lays me down. Clothing flies as we can't get undressed fast enough.

Cool air hits my bare skin as Shidan kisses his way across my stomach. He looks up, meeting my eyes and smiling as he rests his warm hands to either side of my stomach. The smile on his face and the lights dancing in his eyes give away his thoughts before he says them.

"Ours," he says, a soft hiss dragging out the s sound.

Self-conscious, I nod placing my own hands on my stomach.

"My lyutik."

"What does that even mean?" I ask, mildly exasperated that the word doesn't translate.

Shidan cocks his head to one side, his brow furrowing in the most adorable way creating a wrinkle in his scales. It makes me imagine what he'll look like when he's old.

"Buttercup," he says, at last, carefully sounding the word. "It is one of my only remaining memories, a yellow flower… and my mother. It makes me think of being loved."

"Buttercup?" I ask, shaking my head. "You're kidding me, that's it?"

He frowns deeply then nods. "Yes," he says. "Or as close as I can bring it to your language."

Laughter grips me, taking over my body of it's own

accord. I can't stop it. Shidan rises up onto his elbows, staring at me in non-comprehension.

"Good grief," I say, wiping tears away.

"This is funny?" he asks.

"Yeah," I say, trying to catch my breath and still chuckling.

All this time, I see it now, how epically fitting. What a weird world it is. Shidan waits, patient as ever, so much like what he would be in an ancient movie that I haven't seen since I was a kid. My mother loved that movie, played it all the time on the vid screen.

"Why?" he asks, crawling up over me, his warm body covering mine. "I do not understand."

"An old, old movie," I say. "About true love."

"I like love," he says, closing for a kiss.

"I do too," I say, realizing it's true.

"All you need to say now, is 'as you wish'," I tell him, putting a finger to his lips. "And I'll call you Wesley, it'll be perfect."

"Wesley?" he asks, arching an eyebrow. "My name is Shidan."

"Oh yes, but your alter ego will be the Dread Pirate Roberts!" I say, laughter taking over again.

"I do not understand," he says. "I am not a pirate!"

I laugh again. "I know you're not. Maybe we can go and get some vid sticks and players, eventually."

"What is a 'vid stick'," he asks.

"When they built the ship it was loaded down with entertainment from my home planet. We didn't have facilities to produce new content so it's all stuff from old Earth. Books, movies, etc. The entertainment comes on small sticks that you plug in or call up on a player and watch. It's moving pictures."

"Moving pictures?" he asks, frowning again.

"Did you not have television and movies before the devastation?"

"I guess not, I don't know what these are," he says. "We had holo-shows, perhaps they are similar?"

"Perhaps, makes sense, you'd call them something different," I say.

Grabbing him around his neck I pull him in close and kiss him. Happiness wells up like a bubbling brook starting in my core and climbing until my throat clamps shut. He presses against me, making me feel whole in ways I didn't know I needed. Emotions, too strong for words, make my limbs tremble. Here is everything I needed and wanted in my life but didn't know was missing.

"Lyutik," he says, breaking our kiss. He wipes my tear away, concern so clear on his face it melts my heart further. "What is it?"

Shaking my head, I swallow hard, trying to open my throat. Tears fall because I can't contain the strength of the feelings raging through me.

"I'm sorry," I choke out at last. "I didn't..."

He kisses me when words fail me again. I can't get the thoughts in my head into words. His kisses trail across my lips, down my cheek to my neck then back up and down the other side until he is over me again.

"You are my treasure," he says.

"I know," I say. "I need you to know... to understand."

"Yes, my lyutik," he says.

"Another man loved me," I say. Shidan goes still, eyes boring into mine. I rush the words out, not wanting to hurt him. "I didn't, well we weren't, you know lovers, but he loved me. We worked together, flew together, we were close..."

Tears rise again along with an overwhelming wave of sadness. I thought I'd put all this behind me, damn it.

"Lyutik, it's fine," Shidan says, wiping my tears and kissing me. "I understand."

Somehow, I know he does. His understanding makes it easier, warmer. How did I ever hold him at bay?

"His love for me… he sacrificed himself… for me."

The words fall out of my mouth like a weight and when they do, the guilt that I've harbored goes along with them. I inhale deeply and it's like the first air I've ever had. I'm lighter somehow.

"A noble man," Shidan says.

"No!" I exclaim. "Stupid and don't you ever do it!"

Shidan tilts his head stopping his kisses to look at me directly. "No?"

"No," I say, shaking my head emphatically. "He didn't have to do that. I'd rather he was alive and with me then dead because of me. I can't stand… the idea that you… you'd do the same."

"Of course I would, lyutik," he says, so matter-of-fact it make my breath catch.

"Don't you dare!" I say, tears welling up. "Now that you're mine, don't you ever dare. You LIVE for me, you hear me? You LIVE. Don't you go being all noble and sacrificing your-self to save me because I don't want to live in a world without you. I don't want to raise our child without you. You got that Shidan?"

His smile broadens and he nods. The light dancing in his eyes looks almost like he too has tears, something I don't think a Zmaj is capable of.

"Yes, my lyutik," he says, then grinning bigger still. "As you wish."

Laughing, I shake my head. Shidan kisses my lips then down across my chin and to the hollow of my throat. His hands circle my breasts as he kisses his way between them down to my stomach. He kisses his way around it then circles it again and again with tiny kisses and drags of his tongue. His hands roam, fingers leaving hot trails of fire. I wiggle and squirm under his touch. My heart pounds into overtime and my pussy grows wetter. One hand trails over my mound piercing my soft lips and I moan, pushing my hips up.

Warmth burns in my stomach as he teases me. Shidan moves lower than his tongue is teasing my opening, piercing my folds, seeking my clit. When he finds it I scream his name in pleasure and surprise. His rough tongue drags across my sensitive nub, my pulse pounds in response as he lavishes me with his mouth and tongue. Alternatively he sucks then licks, and it's driving me mad.

Grabbing his head I pull him in close. He doesn't stop. Relentless as he drives his tongue deep into my pussy then slides it up across my clitoris. I trail my hands around his head. His love and attention fills me with warmth.

He pushes me up to an edge then I'm falling over. I clench my thighs around his head as crashing waves of pleasure wrack my body. When it passes through and my muscles unclench I fall back into the blankets and breathe heavily.

"I love you," I exhale, then Shidan is here, his tongue drives into my mouth.

His first cock slides in, he doesn't wait to take what he needs. I'm so wet that even with his enormous girth we don't need to go slow. We kiss, our tongues working, then he pulls back and thrusts in again. He groans his pleasure into my mouth.

He pistons in and out faster and faster. No considerations to time, noise, or anything that is not the pleasure of our moment, the love we share.

I rise to meet each thrust and retreat in time. My heart pounds and I feel his fall into time with mine, his second heart like an echo as our chests press into each other while

MIRANDA MARTIN

our hips join. I break the kiss to breathe and he rises onto his forearms driving in faster. It's too much. His eyes close, his head arches back.

"Amara," he groans as he thrusts deep into me.

"Shidan!" I cry.

I feel his massive load filling me as his cock pulses over and over pushing his seed deep inside. He collapses on top of me gasping air. Running my fingers down along his back I touch his wings and remember the beautiful, shimmering wings of the baby. They're gorgeous. What color will the scales of our child be? Will it be a boy or a girl? What will we name it?

Shidan's cock softens, and he pulls out, rolling over to lie beside me. My head rests on his arm as I trace the bulging muscles of his chest. He's lying on his side, his tail makes it impossible for him to lie on his back. We kiss, soft, gentle kisses. Trailing my hand down across his rock hard abs I find his second cock already at attention and ready. I smile then kiss my way across his chest and down. Tracing the lines of his abs with my tongue until at last I come to his cock.

I tease the head and he groans then I lick down the soft underside. I grab his balls with one hand and work them while moving up and down his massive dick with my tongue. He moans and shifts under my attention as I work it. I lick down to his balls then suck one of them into my mouth and out before tracing my way back up his shaft where I tease the head again.

He groans. His long arms reach down and tease my nipples while I tease his cock. I roll over and press my ass back into his hardness. Parting my legs he slides into my pussy. He grabs me by my neck and pushes me forward then he pounds in over and over.

My orgasm comes fast and hard.

He thrusts in, bottoming out and I'm falling into an

orgasm so intense I feel my pussy clamping down on his cock and milking it. He spills his seed once more. Every part of my body tenses as the pleasure overloads my senses. I'm torn apart and created anew in my love for him and his for me. We are one.

As it passes, we turn back into each other and cuddle as sleep comes to claim us. .

No matter what the future holds, I know together, we will face it and come out on top.

The End

Keep reading for a special sneak peek at *Dragon's Hope*

PREVIEW: RED PLANET DRAGONS OF TAJSS BOOK 4

DRAGON'S HOPE

Before the generation ship crashed on this desert alien planet I was a Vagrant. Unplanned and unwanted, struggling to survive.

Now we're on Tajss and if not for the natives, seven foot tall dragon-men with wings and tails and scales, we'd all be dead.

My new friends are finding love and I couldn't be happier for them but I want to fit in, I want to have a place and a purpose. Strangely enough the only one who might understand is one of those scaled dragon-men.

I wanted comfort and attention but it turns out 'one night stand' doesn't translate into Zmaj. He wants more and won't give up until he claims his treasure. Me.

ASTAROT

I move through the door ahead of her then hear her gasp, turning just in time to see her mouth fall open then she turns a circle. Placing her hands over her mouth she shakes herself then walks towards the edge of the roof.

The view is stunning, which is why I brought her here. The dual red suns are setting on the horizon, peeking over the mountain range in the far distance. Their final, blazing rays cause the sand to sparkle like a perfect gem. Brilliant reds, whites, and arcing lines of blue dance across the rolling dunes towards the city. The dome over the city that keeps out predators filters the light and turns it into a dreamy haze.

"You like it?" I ask.

"Like it? It's... stunning."

My smile is so wide my jaw hurts but I don't care. My scales tingle with excitement because my treasure is pleased. Lana turns towards me, placing her hands on my chest, looking up into my eyes. The warmth of her hands spreads across my scales. She rises and I'm pulled into her like a gravity well until our lips meet. Everything focuses into that singular point of contact where we are becoming one. Her arms move over my shoulders, wrapping around my neck. I put my arms around her waist, pulling her tighter against me. Her body melds to mine as our mating of mouths continues.

Lana pulls back, gasping in air, then she kisses across my jaw. Her hot tongue drags along the line of my neck. My hands drop to her full ass, running over her curves. My first cock stiffens to the point I might explode before we do anything.

The soft mounds of her large breasts press hard against my chest, moving as she does, enticing. Her hips move against mine and I grind into her. Desire rules the day, I want to make her mine. I lift her up, bringing her closer, her legs wrap around my waist. My cock presses against the cloth of my pants, straining for her.

Lana moans as her hips grind against my dick. I pull her

head back from where she is kissing my neck. Our lips come together with bruising force. My grip in her hair holds us together. Her tongue licks my lips then presses past them into my mouth. My tongue rises to meet hers in a dance. Her pussy is so close, grinding against my cock. I need her. Pressure builds in my core until I'm sure I can't wait any longer.

Her hand drives between us until it finds my cock. She works her way into my pants and takes my dick in a firm grip. She strokes up and down. I close my eyes concentrating to avoid the impending explosion. She unwraps her legs so I lower her back to her feet. Pulling her hands out of my pants she runs her hands across my chest. She lowers herself before me, dragging her hands along my body as she does.

In moments my pants are dropping to the ground and my cock springs free. Lana takes it in a hand but her small, human hand isn't big enough to wrap around it. Her light touch strokes the soft underside. Looking up, she smiles, then runs her tongue along my shaft.

"Oh!" I cry out in surprise and pleasure.

New sensations race through my body unlike anything I've felt before. My first load explodes, pumping out onto her and the ground between us as she strokes and runs her tongue along my shaft. She doesn't stop until I'm spent.

"Good?" she asks, rising until her lips are next to mine.

"Beyond," I say.

I work the buttons of her shirt then pull it over her shoulders. When it drops off, I move my head back so I can see her enticing mounds. A Zmaj woman's breasts had hard plates that protected them which opened only for feeding babies. Lana's are out all the time, which is fascinating, and Lana's look larger than the other women's too. I've fantasized about what they might look like under her clothing.

Some kind of white cloth with straps that run over her shoulders covers them still. I slide the straps down but the cloth doesn't drop. She presses her mouth to mine, pulling my attention. Our tongues meet and dance but I continue to explore her beauty with my hands. My second cock is rising, straining between us now, but I ignore it, focusing what attention I can on her breasts.

Hooking my fingers under the cloth that is still protecting them I pull it back. It stretches but doesn't come loose so I pull it down and at last her breasts are exposed. I lower my head. The centers are light brown, circular, with bumps. On instinct I tease them with my tongue then take one in my mouth. A hard point forms so I nibble on that. Lana moans, her hands grabbing my head and holding me tight against her.

Moving over to the other I go back and forth and she groans louder. Keeping most of my attention on her breasts with my hands, I work at her pants until they drop free. One handed I rub between her thighs. Another piece of cloth covers her mound, it feels thin, so I grab the sides and slide it off.

Touching the soft fur that grows on her mound I can feel wetness coming from her. She is ready for mating and I want to, but I hold off. I press one finger into the opening past her soft lips and push it into her wetness. I continue licking and teasing her breasts while exploring her delicate folds with my finger.

"Astarot," she pants, thrusting her hips forward and driving my finger deeper.

She's tight around my finger, gripping it hard, I wonder if I can fit into her without harming her. I know the other Zmaj males have done so, but I don't want to hurt Lana. I will let her lead to be sure I do not harm her.

Her hips thrust back then forward driving my finger in and out so I comply. Moving it faster, she pants louder and louder. I lick her breasts in time with the thrusting of my fingers. My lips lock onto the hard point and pull then switch to the other and repeat.

Her groans become a constant chant of wordless sounds of pleasure. As her body adjusts to my finger inside her, it becomes wetter. I slide a second finger in, expanding her, preparing her for my cock. It slides in easy but again feels tight. She groans as she moves her hips back and forth.

She pulls on the back of my head. I look up and she leans in, pressing her lips to mine and groans into my mouth. As her body adjusts and the wetness increases, I add a third finger. She gasps in surprise but the panting groans continue.

Deciding she is ready I hook my hands under her ass and lift her up. My second cock is ready, throbbing with desire. Moving slow while continuing to kiss I lower her down until I feel the first hints of her wetness touching my cock. She throws her head back and sighs as I continue lowering her.

The head of my cock pushes into her until the first ridge on top of my cock meets resistance. The pressure of her sliding down increases and then with surprising suddenness, the first ridge is enveloped by her tightness. She yelps and I stop, worried.

When she opens her eyes and meets mine, she bites her lower lip then nods. I resume lowering her onto my dick. Nothing has ever felt better. Her body grips me, welcoming me, it's a sensation like coming home after a long, hard day. I groan as I slide deeper into her until at last my cock is buried. The hard ridge at the base on my pelvis probes into her soft folds. She shifts her hips then gasps, her eyes widen, and she smiles.

"Oh god!" Lana exclaims, rotating her hips in a circle.

Her grip on my shoulders tightens. Smashing her lips into mine, our teeth click together, then her tongue is driving into my mouth as she pulls herself up then drops back down on my cock.

She sets a fast, hard rhythm, one I never would have tried. Rising and falling on my dick. My core tightens until it's a hard ball. I'm struggling to maintain my control, she feels so good.

"Astarot," she grunts my name with each downward thrust.

As she lowers herself taking me in, she throws her head back and lets out a wordless cry of pleasure. I answer her cry with my own as we become one. Our bodies joining in the physical manifestation as our souls entwine with each other.

She puts her head on my shoulder, panting. I can feel her pounding heart against my chest. As her heart rate slows and she regains her breath she moves, raising her head and pulling herself up. I assist her, taking her off my cock, and lowering her to the ground.

"That was fun," she smiles.

"Yes," I agree, as we both gather our clothing and dress.

She pulls her shirt on then stops to stare out at the encroaching shadows. The suns have dipped below the horizon, only their reflected light pushes back the darkness.

"It's beautiful," she exhales.

"I think so," I say, stepping over to her and putting an arm around her waist.

"Okay, well I'll see you tomorrow," she says as she turns and walks towards the door.

"Uh, what?" I ask.

The sudden shift in attitude and the words make no sense. We joined, there is much to discuss, what is she doing?

"I'll see you tomorrow?" she asks, confusion obvious on her face.

"But, we joined," I say.

"Yes, and it was fun," she replies.

"I do not understand."

She looks confused too. She shakes her head then tilts it

to one side. "I have to butcher tomorrow. Aren't you going to be there?" she asks.

Butcher? The meat? She's talking about the meat, but what about us?

"But… what about… we joined?" I ask, feeling lost.

"Yes," she says shaking her head. "It's a hook-up. A one night stand, right?"

"A… one night stand?" I've never heard of such a thing. I know the words but putting them together makes no sense.

Dragon's Hope Is Available Now!

ABOUT THE AUTHOR

USA Today Bestselling Author of fantasy and scifi romance, Miranda Martin's books feature larger than life heroes with out-of-this-world anatomy and smart heroines destined to save the world. As a little girl she would sneak off with her nose in a book, dreaming of magical realms. Today she brings those fantasies to life and adores every fan who chooses to live in them for a while.

She was born and raised in southern Virginia, but as a veteran she's traveled to places like Korea, Hawaii and good 'ole Texas. Now she's settled in Kansas, the heart of America, with her husband and daughters. Her favorite animals are dragons, unicorns and cats. If she's not writing, you can still find her tucked away somewhere with a warm blanket and her nose in a book.

Get in touch!
mirandamartinromance.com
miranda@mirandamartinromance.com